Contents

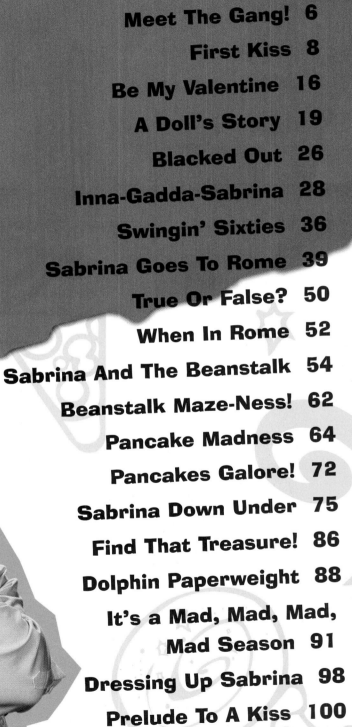

Sabrina
The Teenage Witch™

Annual 2006

Published by Pedigree Books Limited
Beech Hill House, Walnut Gardens, Exeter,Devon, EX4 4DH.
E-mail: books@pedigreegroup.co.uk Published 2005

Pedigree®

visit
Sabrina
The Teenage Witch
www.archiecomics.com

7.99

Meet The Gang!

Hi, everyone! Welcome to my fifth fantastic annual. It`s filled with great stories of some of my early adventures as a witch, and my amazing globe-trotting travels to Rome and Australia! There`s also lots of cool activities to make-and-do! But in case you`ve been lost in the Other Realm for awhile, let me give you a quick run-down of all my family and friends!

Sabrina Spellman

First, of course, there`s me. I discovered I was a witch when I turned 16 - and what a crazy birthday present that turned out to be. As you`ll see, it took me awhile to get the hang of witchcraft...my first attempts were a bit of a disaster! As most of you know, I live in Westbridge, Massachusettes, which is near Boston. My mom, Diana Spellman, is a mortal, off on an archaeological dig in Peru and my dad, Edward, is a warlock, exploring the fourth dimension. The Witches` Council has a stupid rule about witches not marrying mortals that basically says, when I got my powers, I couldn't see my mom again - or she'd be turned into a ball of wax! With my Dad busy in the Other Realm, they sent me to live with...

Hilda & Zelda Spellman

My two fun-loving Aunts! They`re really cool, if both a bit wacky. Aunt Zelda is a serious scientist, but she once dated Merlin the Magician, so she's not always seroius. Aunt Hilda is more of a fun-loving free-spirit who gets into almost as much trouble as I do. She had an on-again-off-again relationship with Drell, head of the Witches` Council. But, she finally found her soulmate, Will, in the Other Realm Shopping Mall. Don't ask.

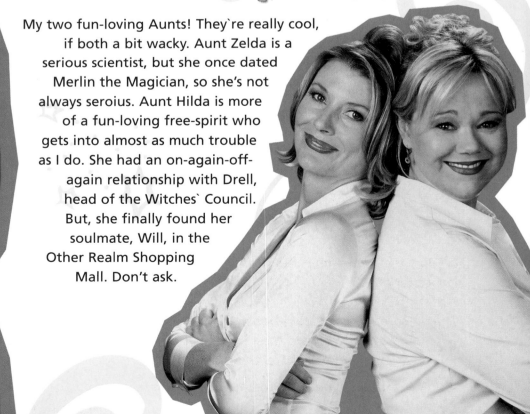

Salem Saberhagan

My wise-cracking, talking cat! (All teenagers should have one!) I love Salem, even though he does drive me crazy at times. He acts tough and streetwise, but really he`s a big softy, and an even bigger scaredy-cat. Salem is actually a warlock who was turned into a cat for 100 years for trying to take over the world! (That definitely sounds like Salem!) Now he spends his days surfing the Internet and making purchases using my aunts` credit cards! He just doesn't know how to stay out of trouble!

Harvey Kinkle

SWOON! Harvey`s both my best male friend and on-off boyfriend. More on than off, thank goodness, but hey, I`m a teenager. We both went out with other people over the years - but somehow Harvey and I always got back together. Harvey loves playing football (although he`s usually just warming the bench), hockey (where he's actually a star - maybe he should have tried playing football on ice!), and riding his motorcycle. We`ve recently discovered that we really are Soul Mates - and I wouldn`t want it any other way!

Valerie Kirckhead

My best friend in high school, I even got to tell her I was a witch one Friday the 13th. Only because she would forget it at midnight though. Crazy things were always happening around Val, but she never seemed to mind. A sure sign of a true friend!

Josh

I met Josh when he managed the Coffee House, where I worked part-time after school. I have to admit, I developed a big crush on him! Then, when he decided he liked me, I didn't like him, but when I decided I did like him after all, he was already dating someone else. My life is very complicated sometimes. We finally got in sync when I was in collage and he got a job as a photographer at the *Boston Citizen* newspaper where he got me a job as an intern and helped me start my journalistic career!

Dreama

As you`ll discover, later in this annual, once I finally received my Witch's Licence (oooh, that was hard work!), the Witches` Council assigned me another teenage witch to tutor. Dreama had been neglecting her magic, so her parents sent her to the Mortal Realm to study. But, no matter how hard she tries, her magic never lasts, or worse, goes completely wrong! (Been there, done that, got the bruises to prove it!)

Well, that`s all you need to know! Now turn the page and let the magic begin!

First Kiss

Original story written by Renee Phillips & Carrie Honigblum

What`s one of the most exciting events in a young teenage girl`s life? That`s right! Her first kiss! And I was looking forward to having my first kiss with Harvey!

It all started a few months after I had found out that I was a witch. I was still a student at Westbridge High School, and Harvey and I had grown pretty close. So close that we even exchanged Valentine Day cards.

I had worked hard on my card. It was large and elaborately decorated. Harvey`s on the other hand was…well, a very small heart cut out of red construction paper.

"Wow, yours is so big," said Harvey, obviously embarrassed.

"And yours is so…cute," I said, trying to make him feel better.

Harvey shrugged. "My Valentine started out as big as yours, but I kept trying to make it even and it got smaller and smaller."

"But I love it," I told him. "It`s very symmetrical."

"I love symmetry," said Harvey, smiling. "Things just look nicer that way. Like your face. "He leaned closer towards me. "It`s really symmetrical."

But before anything romantic could develop, the rotten school bell rang! Gurrr!

9

Harvey walked me home to my Aunt Zelda and Aunt Hilda's house, after school. They were out at a museum, but Salem was in the kitchen, surfing the Internet.

I told him to stay out of the way, while I entertained Harvey.

"Like I don`t have anything better to do than spy on her," muttered Salem after I had returned to the living room. "Wait, I don`t." And he snuck upstairs to watch.

Harvey and I were sat close together, flicking through a book on the coffee table when our hands brushed. To both our surprise, sparks flew!

"Uh, oh," groaned Salem on the stairs. "Sparks are flying."

Harvey decided he didn`t want to look at a book anymore.

"What do you want to do?" I asked, hopefully.

And then he said the magic words. "Kiss you?"

Heart pounding, I moved in for my first kiss. Eyes closed, our lips were just about to touch, when...

"Meow!"

Salem dove in and landed between us, completely ruining the moment!

Furious, I scooped him up and carried him into the kitchen, tossing him onto the table.

"You can`t kiss Harvey," Salem said, before I could strangle him. "Something horrible could happen. The sparks were a warning."

"What?" I panicked. "He could burst into flames?"

"No," said Salem. "Worse."

I couldn`t believe it. How could this be happening to me??!

"Okay," I said, breathing deeply. "I won`t kiss Harvey. But if you`re making this up, I swear you will be neutered. Slowly."

I got rid of Harvey by telling him I had to take Salem to the vet. When Aunt Hilda and Aunt Zelda arrived home, I demanded they tell me why I couldn`t kiss Harvey!

"It`s actually quite simple," said Aunt Zelda. "When a witch kisses a mortal for the first time, the mortal turns into a frog."

Nooo! "You mean, I can never kiss Harvey?"

Well, it was and it wasn`t.

"There`s a fifty percent chance it`s good news," said Aunt Hilda. "And fifty percent chance it`s bad."

It was kind of like a coin toss. So I started tossing a coin to see what my chances were. Out of one hundred tries, it came up fifty heads and fifty tails!

And then Harvey arrived to take me to the movies. When I consulted my Aunts, they said they could see no reason why two <u>friends</u> couldn`t go see a movie.

"Right," I groaned. "Two friends." So there we were in the theatre, watching some dumb action flick, when Harvey couldn`t wait any longer. He leaned over to kiss me! Pulling away in panic, I pointed at the tub of popcorn he was holding. POOF! The popcorn popped out of the tub.

"I need more popcorn," I said, leaping out of my seat. Boy, that was close!

From then on, every time he tried to kiss me, I found a way to get out of it. Disappointed, Harvey dropped me back home.

"Sabrina," he said, as we sat in his car outside my Aunts house. "Maybe I`m reading too much into this, but yesterday I got the feeling you wanted to kiss me. And today I feel like you don`t. If that`s what you want, we can just be...friends."

I was sooo frustrated. I wanted to be more than friends, too, but I couldn`t tell him that because...because...oh, what the heck?

Grabbing hold of Harvey, I planted a kiss on him. We broke away. I held my breath.

"You`re still here!" I squealed with relief.

Harvey smiled. "I`ll always be here for you, Sabri- - "

There was a blinding flash. And Harvey turned into a frog!

"Ribbet," he croaked.

"Not without transmogrifying him," said Aunt Zelda.

This could not be worse! I hated being a witch!

I was lying on my bed in the dark, when my Aunts came in. Aunt Zelda turned on the light.

"We`ve been doing some research," said Aunt Hilda, holding up the Witches Handbook.

"Since you`re half-mortal," Aunt Zelda explained. "There`s only a fifty-fifty chance that Harvey will turn into a frog."

"So that`s good news?" I asked, hopefully.

"There's still hope," said Aunt Zelda after I had burst into the house with Harvey-the-Frog.

"The true love clause!" beamed Aunt Hilda, realising what she meant. "There's a test you can take to determine if it's true love, and if it is, Harvey will change back into a person."

"And if it isn't?" I asked, nervously.

"You'll be changed into a frog," Aunt Hilda finished.

I mean, Harvey was super-cute and I really, really liked him, but how did I know it was true love?

My Aunts gave me a quick pop quiz: did I think about Harvey when he wasn't around? Check! Did my heart beat faster when I saw him? Check! Did it bother me when he chewed gum? Er…no. Check!

"Then it might be true love!" declared Aunt Hilda.

"I'm taking the test!" I said.

We took the linen closet (gateway to the Other Realm) to the National Institute of Love. It was totally over-decorated in love hearts.

"Normally it's very clinical," said Aunt Zelda. "But they go all out for Valentine's Day." As we passed through a door, our clothes changed colours to shades of pink and red. Freaky!

Sitting down on a love seat, I put the shoebox containing Harvey-the-Frog on a coffee table.

"Drell should be here any minute," said Aunt Hilda. "And it's kind of strange we're seeing each other today. You know, it's the ninety-fourth anniversary of our thirty-second break-up."

Drell was Head of the Witches Council. He and Aunt Hilda had an on-off relationship that had lasted for centuries.

"So Sabrina," he said when he finally arrived. "You're here to take the Test of True Love? There are three parts to the test. Each one more horrifying than the last."

Gee, I couldn`t wait.

After signing the standard release form, I was shown three doors. Stepping through door number one, I found myself on the sound stage of a game show. And dressed in a Mod Sixties outfit!

"And let`s meet our next contestant," announced a retro Sixties game show host from his podium. "Sabrina Spellman!"

"What is this?" I asked, puzzled.

"Part one of the test," he explained. "It`s the True Love Game!"

As canned applause rang out, the game show host ushered me to a chair which was next to his podium. A partition stood between me and three Harveys`, all dressed in different coloured leisure suits.

The name of the game was to find out how well I knew the person I thought I was in love with.

I started reading out some really dumb questions I`d been given to ask the Harveys. And each of their answers was even dumber than the questions!

I`d about had it when I got to "What`s your favourite kind of triangle?" These stupid questions weren`t telling me anything!

"No one said the test would be easy," said the game show host.

The first Harvey said his favourite triangle was obtuse - even though he didn`t know why. The second Harvey liked scalene triangles. But Harvey number three said equilateral.

"I like that it`s symmetrical," he said.

I remembered what my Harvey said to me at school!

"That's him!" I squealed excitedly. "That's my Harvey! Harvey number three!"

"You're right, Sabrina!" yelled the game show host as canned applause rang out. "You've passed part one!"

I stepped out of Door Number One to be warmly greeted by Aunt Hilda and Aunt Zelda.

"You've passed the Test of Friendship," said Drell. "And true love can't exist without friendship."

"I'm pumped," I said excitedly. "What's next?"

"Door Number Two."

I headed for the door. "Wish me luck, Harvey," I said.

"Ribbet," croaked Harvey-the-Frog.

Stepping through Door Number Two, there was a blinding flash, and I found myself sitting in one of two chaise lounges beside a pool, dressed in swimwear and sunglasses. A gorgeous young guy named Zak sat down on the other chaise lounge.

He started telling me how pretty I was, and tempting me with chocolate cake. I almost fell for it, too!

"Wait!" I suddenly realised. "You're trying to make me forget Harvey, aren't you? I can't eat cake when Harvey's in trouble."

"Yes, you can," said Zak.

"No, I can't."

"Eat it!" Zak growled.

"No!" I cried.

There was more canned applause. I had passed the second test!

"Nicely done," said Drell, when I exited Door Number Two. "You passed the Test of Fidelity."

"You resisted temptation," explained Aunt Zelda. Something that tests every relationship."

The last test was so dangerous, I was expected to fail, so I had to choose what kind of frog I wanted to be when it was all over.

"Good luck. And don't be nervous," Aunt Zelda said encouragingly as I tried to open Door Number Three.

"Push, don't pull," Drell yawned as if I was already a stupid frog.

I found myself standing beside the edge of a firey chasm, dressed in a flowing gown. There was a forked sign nearby. One side read `True Love`, which pointed to a rickety bridge over the chasm. The other side read `Safe Road`, which pointed in the other direction. Far on the other side of the chasm stood Harvey.

"It`s a test of faith," Harvey called to me. "You have to get to me."

"Is the `Safe Road` anywhere near you?" I asked hopefully.

"No, I think it dead-ends in the suburbs," he answered.

"Then there`s only one way," I said, starting to cross over the bridge. Suddenly, I screamed. The bridge began to collapse!

"Turn back!" cried Harvey. "It`s not worth it!"

I looked at Harvey. "Yes, it is!" I said, determinedly. "I can do this!"

I took a few steps back, ran and jumped! Flying through the air as the bridge collapsed completely, I landed on the very edge of the chasm. I struggled to get my balance. If I fell, it

would be goodbye Sabrina!

Just before I toppled backwards, Harvey grabbed my arm and pulled me to safety! Phew!

"I made it!" I gasped. "Oh, Harvey!"

We hugged...and Harvey disappeared!

"All that for a hologram?" I groaned.

I stepped out triumphantly through Door Number Three.

"I did it!" I cheered. "I passed! It is true love!"

But to my surprise, Harvey was still a frog!

"To change him back," explained Aunt Zelda. "You have to return to the scene of the kiss and kiss him again."

Kiss a frog? Uggh! Gross!

We returned to Westbridge and I took Harvey-the-Frog back to his car outside my Aunts` house. Only moments had passed in the Mortal Realm (time is weird in the Other Realm!).

I held up Harvey-the-frog to my face. "Your lips are all slimy," I said, almost gagging.

I closed my eyes and kissed the frog.

And the frog changed back to Harvey!

"This is great!" I said, as we finished our very first proper kiss. "Could we try again? I think I`d enjoy it more this time."

We kissed again...and outside the car, fireworks exploded in the night sky! Now that`s what I call true love!

Be My Valentine!

Helllp! Some of my family and friends have sent me Valentine Day cards, but my magic`s gone loopy and mixed-up their names! Can you unscramble the letters to find out who sent me what card?

1

2

3

4

5

6

7

Answers: 1: HILDA SPELLMAN, 2: VALERIE BIRCHHEAD, 3: WILLARD KRAFT, 4: QUIZMASTER, 5: SALEM SABERHAGEN, 6: ZELDA SPELLMAN, 7: HARVEY KINKLE

A Doll's Story

Original story written by
Carrie Honigblum & Renee Phillips

Hi, cat fans! It`s your favourite feline, Salem! I bet most of you are looking forward to the day when you get paid for babysitting, right? Well, a word of warning...it`s not always as easy as it looks!

Take Sabrina, for instance. When Marigold called, she jumped at the chance to watch her cousin Amanda for one night - and a hundred bucks. She`d obviously forgotten what a brat that kid could be.

"I think I can handle a nine-year old," she proclaimed when we all tried to stop her.

"Sabrina," said Aunt Zelda. "You`re half-mortal. Amanda`s a full witch."

But her words fell on deaf ears. "Amanda says we`re going to be having fun before I know it," Sabrina said, hanging up the phone. Then a huge smile appeared magically on her face that wouldn`t go away, no matter how hard she tried.

"Oh, dear," sighed Aunt Zelda. "Amanda was able to do that all the way from the Other Realm."

Sabrina didn`t know what she was in for!

19

Everyone gathered around the linen closet. A lot of inter-Realm travel went on that day, and yet the cat still went nowhere. As soon as Amanda arrived, Aunt Zelda and Aunt Hilda headed off together to a witches spa - they had been arguing a lot lately and wanted some time away from each other. Yeah, yeah, I know that doesn`t make sense, but the spa was having a two-for-one special. Go figure!

Amanda came through the door, pulling a large toy box on wheels.

"My toy box," she told Sabrina. "I never leave home without it."

Sabrina was determined to prove her Aunts wrong about her being able to control Amanda. She kept smiling, even after Amanda rolled over her foot with that toy box. Accidents can happen, right?

Amanda is no accident. She`s a fully-fledged train wreck!

I was catnapping on Sabrina`s bed when the girls came in. Sabrina had some crayons and a colouring book to keep Amanda occupied. But Amanda wanted to play with a glass jewellery box.

"Oh, no, please put that down," said Sabrina. "Harvey gave it to me."

She pointed and the jewellery box floated out of Amanda`s hand.

"But I`m the guest," growled Amanda, pointing, and the box started to float back to her.

"Amanda, I asked you nicely," said Sabrina sternly. "Give it to me."

A magical tug-o`-war began, the jewellery box being pulled first one way, and then the other.

And then it dropped onto the floor, shattering! CRASSH!

"Okay," said Amanda. "You can have it."

Then she saw me. "Oooh, kitty," she giggled. "You want to play?"

"I don`t do 'play'," I hissed.

"But you`re so small," she said. "I like things big."

Amanda pointed, and turned me into a large panther! I let out a loud ROOOAAAR!

"Amanda, he`s not declawed," panicked Sabrina. "Turn him back!"

And thankfully, she did. Whew!

It all went downhill from there.

I got a break when Sabrina`s friend Valerie came over, and Amanda got her to play cards with them.

"I win! I win!" cheered

to play with," she suggested to Amanda.

Amanda smiled. "Good idea."

Pointing, she turned Sabrina into a stiff, plastic doll, with a gingham dress, apron and Mary Jane shoes!

"We`re going to have so much fun," Amanda giggled, swinging her Sabrina doll by one arm as she started upstairs, accidentally banging Sabrina`s head against every spoke of the banister as she went!

Well, Sabrina`s Aunts did try to warn her!

And she wasn`t the only one Amanda zapped! A few minutes later, Sabrina sat at a children`s table having a tea party with Amanda - and me! I was now wearing a bonnet and frilly blouse!

"This is so humiliating," groaned Sabrina the doll, after Amanda had left to get some more crumpets.

"You?" I growled. "I`m wearing pantaloons."

When Amanda returned, Sabrina told her that we had all had a lot of fun - yeah, right! - but to turn her back, and she would help Amanda to get ready for bed.

"I`m not going to bed," giggled Amanda, picking her up and crossing over to the toy box. "You`re going to bed. And Salem and I are going to stay up and play." Noooo!

With that, she put Sabrina inside the toy box and closed the lid!

Amanda, after winning game after game.

Valerie was amazed. "She always has the right cards. It`s like magic or something."

While Sabrina went to answer a knock at the door, Amanda told Valerie a little something of herself.

"I live in the fourth galaxy of the Other Realm," she explained. "Where`re you from?"

Thinking Amanda was playing make-believe, Valerie answered, "I`m from a big castle in Never-Never Land."

Amanda snorted. "You`re delusional."

Once Valerie had left, Sabrina wanted to clean up the mess Amanda seemed to leave everywhere she went. "I bet you have a nice doll

Sabrina found herself on the floor of the toy box. A big teddy bear wearing a `Hug Me` heart around his neck approached her,

"Welcome to the box," he said bitterly.

"Who are you?" asked Sabrina.

"I was an ice cream man," explained the bear, who`s name was Ralphie. "Then I told Amanda we were out of chocolate."

Looking around, Sabrina saw lots of mismatched toy furniture, arranged as if people lived there. Toy flashlights set up as floor lamps supplied the light.

Ralphie introduced her to some other people who had been turned into toys. There was Carol, who used to be Amanda`s hairdresser. Now she too was a plastic doll.

And Amanda`s dentist, Doctor Rafkin, who had

been turned into an action figure, complete with a superhero`s spandex costume and cape.

"Well Sabrina," said Ralphie, once she had explained that she was Amanda`s babysitter. "You`re never getting out of here. None of us are ever getting out of here."

"I can figure this out. I just have to use my --" Sabrina tapped her temple. "Rubber head?"

"Amanda, I have to go to the bathroom," Sabrina told her, figuring she would think of a way to change back once she was out of the box.

Amanda snorted. "You`re not a Betsy-Wetsy!" And slammed down the lid!

Ralphie stared at Sabrina. "You`re not a Bertsy-Wetsy, are you?" he asked, worriedly.

Rubber or not, that head had a good brain - and no time to lose. "I`ve got it!" She knocked on the side of the box, calling. "Amanda! Amanda!"

Amanda opened the lid of the box, staring down at Sabrina.

"What?" snarled Amanda, who was riding on my back. "I`m playing giddy-up with Salem."

"Poison, please," I cried. I couldn`t take any more of the little brat! "Someone feed me poison."

Sabrina thought she had problems! Downstairs in the living room, Amanda had zapped in a seesaw. She sat on one end and stuck me on the other. The seesawing was relentless. Up and down, and…and…I thought I`d toss my tea and crumpets on the next wave down!

That would have been better than what really happened.

Amanda suddenly came down really hard, and I was catapulted high into the air!

"I hate my life!!!!" I screamed, before crashing painfully to the floor.

Inside the toy box, Carol was explaining to Sabrina that they had all managed to get out of the box before.

"Really?" asked Sabrina, hopefully.

"Yeah," muttered Doctor Rafkin. "The problem is you`re still ten inches tall. And real easy to step on."

"I spent two weeks inside a vacuum cleaner once," grumbled Ralphie.

Sabrina looked at a toy phone. "Oh, why doesn`t that phone work?"

"I do," said the phone, much to Sabrina`s surprise. "I was Amanda`s next door neighbour."

Sabrina began to dial. "I`ll just call my aunts and they`ll fix everything," she told the others.

Just then, the Quizmaster appeared. When a witch turned seventeen, she had to take regular tests to get her witch`s licence. The Quizmaster kept turning up out of the blue to test Sabrina.

"Great!" said Sabrina. "You can fix everything!"

"No, I can`t," said the Quizmaster. "I`m here to give you a quiz for your witch`s licence."

"I`m never going to be happy to see you, am I?" Sabrina groaned.

This time, Sabrina`s quiz was to get everyone out of the box. By herself. "Isn`t learning fun?" chuckled the Quizmaster, before disappearing again.

Frustrated, Sabrina laid down on a bed - and her eyes closed shut!

"I`m blind!" she screamed, terrified.

"Sit up," Carol told her. "You`re just not used to your doll eyes."

Sabrina sat up and her eyes opened again. "Okay, that`s better," she said, relieved.

"Way to go," snorted Ralphie to Carol. "That could have kept us entertained for at least a minute."

After giving it a bit more thought, Sabrina had come up with a plan. And she would need all the toys to help her.

"Power to the toys!" she chanted. "Power to the toys!"

Everyone else just stared at her.

"Okay," said Sabrina, embarrassed. "Let`s just get to work."

Meanwhile, Amanda`s next game for us to play was `cat hospital`. She was prowling for me, carrying a giant-sized cotton swab she had created.

"Somebody needs their ears cleaned," she purred. Gulp. Thank goodness I was stealthily stashed in a backpack, hanging on the door inside Sabrina`s closet!

"What else can I do with this?" Amanda said, looking at the giant cotton swab. Using it as a pool cue, she knocked a knickknack from Sabrina`s desk. It smashed onto the floor! CRRASSH!

Before Amanda could wreck anything else, she heard laughter coming from inside the toy box.

Curious, she opened the lid.

"Party!" she could hear a toy shouting. "You`re missing the fun!" another told her.

Amanda sneered. "Oh, please. I`ve had enough therapy to know not to fall for reverse psychology."

She was about to close the lid, when she noticed the result of Sabrina`s big plan - a jack-in-the-box that Sabrina and the other toys had been busy making all afternoon.

"A new toy?" squealed Amanda, excitedly, picking it up. "Where`d this come from? It`s kind of small."

So she pointed, and zapped the jack-in-the-box to giant size.

"Bigger`s always better," she giggled, turning the crank on the side of the box.

A jack-in-the-box version of `Pop Goes the Weasel` rang out, much to Amanda`s delight. The lid popped open…and a full-sized Sabrina, dressed in her normal clothes, jumped out!

"Now it`s my turn to play," she growled at Amanda.

"Oh, yeah?" Amanda growled back. She was about to point, when Sabrina beat her to it! You go, girl!

Amanda`s hands were suddenly behind her back, little pink `finger cuffs`

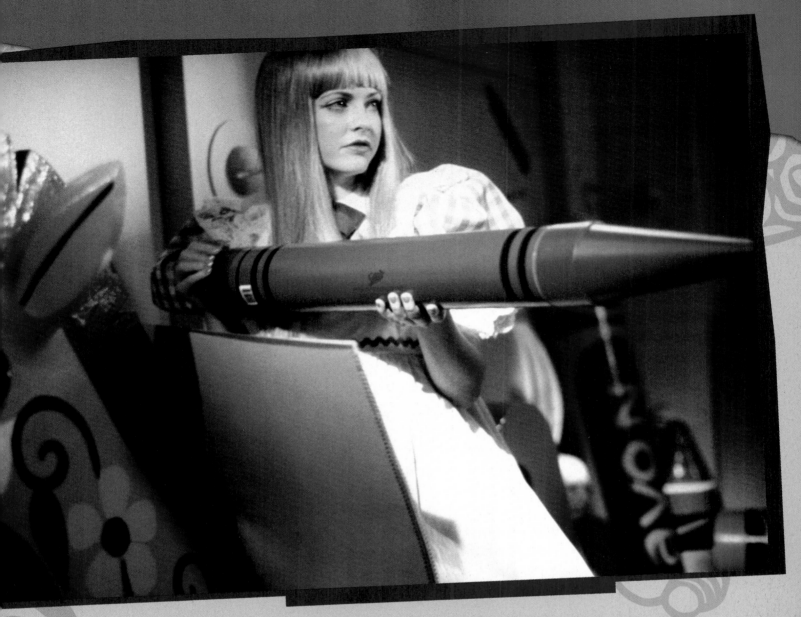

attached to her pointing fingers.

"I'm going to have my mom stop payment on your cheque," Amanda wailed, struggling to escape.

The Quizmaster appeared. "Once again you got yourself out of the mess you got yourself into," he said.

"I'll take that as a `well done`," laughed Sabrina, knowing that she had passed the quiz.

"Hey guys," said Sabrina to the toys, once the Quizmaster had left. "Gather your accessories. You're going home!"

Loud cheers rang from the toy box!

Amanda had to change the toys back to people again. When they had all gone back to the Other Realm, Sabrina gave a deep sigh of relief.

"You know, maybe I shouldn't babysit anymore," she told me.

"You think?" I answered sarcastically.

Aunt Zelda and Aunt Hilda arrived home. The spa trip hadn't worked much magic. They were still arguing!

"Amanda's fine," Sabrina told them, not that they were listening. "She's upstairs asleep."

Later, in her bedroom, Sabrina was at her desk studying while I was relaxing on the bed.

From inside the toy box, we could hear a tiny Amanda ranting. (Yes, Sabrina had paid her back - big time!)

"Sabrina," Amanda screeched. "You'd better do as I say! I want water! Now!"

"Okay, said Sabrina, taking a glass of water from her desk. She opened up the box lid and tossed it in. SPLOOSH!

"Thank you," said Amanda sweetly, realising she would never be set free until she learned some manners.

"I do love a happy ending," I chuckled.

Blacked Out!

Mee-ooow! That rotten Amanda has been causing trouble with her magic again! She`s turned all the doll pictures on Sabrina`s laptop screen into silhouettes! Can you find which two of the dolls are exactly the same?

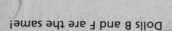

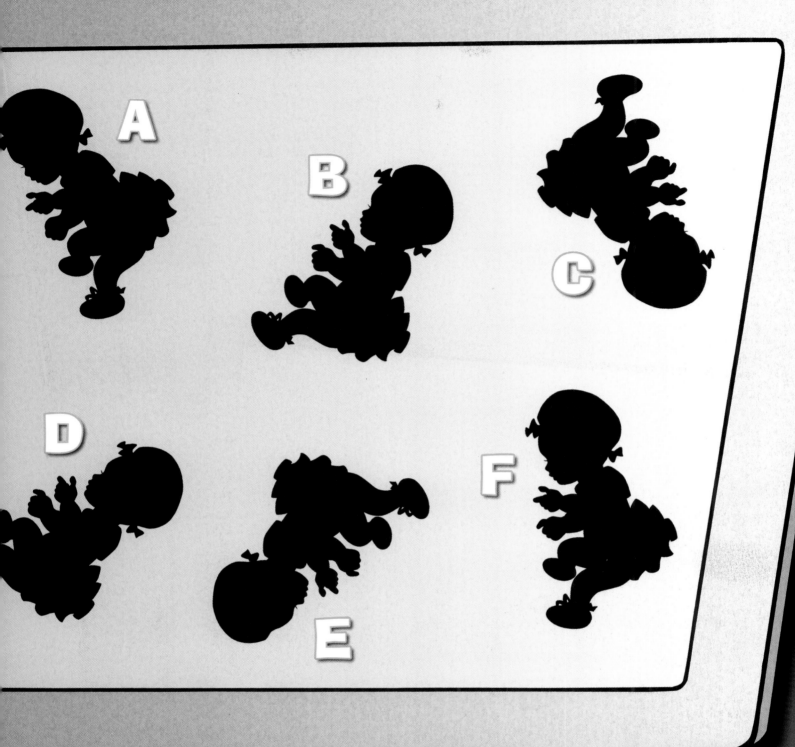

Inna-Gadda Sabrina

Original story written by Sheldon Bull

Zelda here. Let's talk time travel. Always tricky, and usually gives you a headache. Sabrina found out just how much trouble it can be when she took a trip back to the Swingin` Sixties!

It all started innocently enough one night when we were having dinner. As usual, Salem was complaining that he was hungry, even though he'd already had more than enough to eat. He was becoming one fat cat.

"No offence," Hilda told him. "But you`re turning into a furry blimp."

Salem jumped down from the table and headed for the porch. His indignant exit would have been highly effective, and even dramatic if he hadn't gotten stuck in the cat door!

"You laugh, you die," he threatened.

That was it! Time for the cat to go on a diet.

The next morning, Hilda was looking for a pair of pants she hadn't worn in years, Salem was looking for more food, and Sabrina was just looking for clarification.

"Where are my Landlubber bells?" Hilda asked as she joined us for breakfast.

"Refrigerator?" Sabrina said, puzzled, looking at me. "What is she talking about?"

"Landlubbers," explained Hilda excitedly.

"The classic bellbottom pants I wore at the San Francisco Be-In during the Summer of Love in the Age of Aquarius."

"The Sixties," I said, answering Sabrina's blank look. "I'm sorry, Hilda. I threw those pants out years ago. You never wore them."

"I've been waiting thirty years for hip-huggers to come back in. Now they're back, and my hips remain unhugged," Hilda whined.

After all of Salem's pouting about food, the last thing we needed that morning was more whining."

"Can't you just buy another pair?" Sabrina wondered.

"No," wailed Hilda. "That company went out when straight legs came in."

Luckily for Sabrina, it was time for her to head to school. "Sorry about your bell-hugger hips," she sincerely told Hilda, as she looked for her lunch. She found it half-eaten and hidden in a drawer behind a pulchritudinous puss...Salem!

Things at school weren't much better.

Sabrina's English teacher, Mrs. Reilly, had finally had her baby and was off on maternity leave. Mr. Kraft would be taking over her class for six weeks, and Mr. Kraft was never good news for Sabrina.

"I'd say good morning," he muttered in his usual sour tone to the class. "But I work at a public high school, so there are no good mornings for me."

He gave the students `The Waging of War,`, and announced there would be a quiz on the six hundred and fifty pages book the next day.

"At least we only have to read the first three chapters," offered Harvey, when he met Sabrina later in the school cafeteria.

"It only has four chapters," Sabrina pointed out.

They were joined by Sabrina's best friend, Valerie, who was complaining that the school never changed the one flavour of frozen yogurt. When Sabrina politely asked a cafeteria worker if it were possible to get other flavours, she was greeted with angry disdain.

"Why do we bother expressing our opinions when no one ever listens to us," she grumbled.

After lunch, Sabrina's algebra teacher, Mrs Quick, reminded everyone to visit the College Fair that would be in the gym all week. "Everyone can have a rewarding career, regardless of colour or gender, but not if you're an uneducated dolt," she told them.

Visiting the fair, Sabrina took an interest in Franklin & Lee, one of the oldest colleges in America, with a long tradition of academic excellence. The recruiter thought she might be Franklin & Lee material, so she brought an information pack home to show me and Hilda.

"Hilda," I said sadly. "Our little girl is thinking about college. She'll be leaving us soon."

"Never to be seen again," said Hilda, equally sad. "Just like my bellbottoms." The woman is like a broken record.

Upstairs in her room, Sabrina was startled by the appearance of her Quizmaster, who gave her another assignment. She had to pass all of his tests to get her witch's licence. He told her this time, she had to brew up something from the new home supplement of her magic book.

The Quizmaster handed Sabrina something that looked like a glossy women's magazine. Inside, Sabrina found a recipe for a `Time Ball`, and two female witch chefs to help her make one. They told Sabrina the Time Ball wasn't to be eaten, though. So, why did she need chefs? Who knows? Anyway, as we more mature witches know, when a Time Ball is prepared correctly, the person holding it, can change their surroundings to whatever decade they think of.

So Sabrina quickly got to work on my labtop and moulded a Time Ball .It looked like a clay golf ball, but, "It smells like sardines," she said wrinkling her nose.

"Well, if it smells like sardines, then you made it right," the witch chef assured her.

"Okay, then I can go get Aunt Hilda's jeans," laughed Sabrina, holding the ball and thinking hard. "Sixties, here I come."

There was a magical flash of light, and Sabrina found herself dressed like a love child from the Sixties, in a long white kaftan with an embroidered red rim!

be happy to barter if you have any sketches or poetry."

"All I have is money," shrugged Sabrina.

The Hippie clerk looked shocked. "Wow, that is such a metaphor," she said.

Using the Time Ball again, Sabrina returned to the present. Hilda was delighted with her bellbottoms.

"I wondered why we were in the Sixties a minute ago," I said, after Sabrina explained about the Time Ball. I told her only witches knew that time had changed. Mortals were under the spell and thought that whatever they did or saw was normal.

Sabrina headed off to her room. She'd had a busy day between school, regular homework, witch homework and time travel. After she had gone to sleep, a hungry Salem entered.

"Do I smell sardines?" he said, sniffing the air. The perpetually hungry cat leapt onto Sabrina's desk, where he saw the Time Ball.

"This doesn't look like sardines," he muttered. "Oh, who cares."

And Salem ate the Time Ball! Then, as cats do, settled in for a nice, 16-hour nap.

He must have been dreaming about the 1960's because the next morning Sabrina awoke dressed in a floral print nightie under her floral print bedspread. Her headboard and walls were also covered in floral prints!

When she opened her closet to get dressed for school, she pulled out the same white Sixties kaftan she had worn at the boutique the day before.

"Groovy," she giggled.

The Quizmaster appeared, wearing a dashiki and an Afro haircut. "Made a Time Ball, huh? Guess you passed."

Sabrina quickly made her way to a clothes boutique, which, like everything else, now looked like it had in 1967!

She took a pair of jeans from the rack. They had thirty-inch flares and were liberally patched with bright colourful flowers.

"Far out," said the hippie clerk behind the counter when Sabrina went to pay for them. "I'd

"Where did this come from?" she wondered. Then she noticed all her other clothes had changed into Sixties outfits!

"How'd I get back in the Sixties?" she gasped, rushing to her desk, upon which was now an antique typewriter instead of her laptop. Her heart sank as she realised the Time Ball had gone!

"Oh, no," she groaned. "Bummer!"

Quickly dressing in a beige sweater and skirt, suede knee boots, fringed smock and headband, Sabrina rushed downstairs to tell us. Go with the flow, I say.

Hilda and I sat cross-legged on cushions at a low kitchen table. Hilda was happily wearing her beloved bellbottoms.

"Something's wrong," Sabrina said breathlessly.

Hilda shook her head. "Something's only wrong if you believe it's wrong."

"Heavy," I said.

Dragging us upstairs, Sabrina explained about the missing Time Ball. If we didn't find it we'd be stuck in the Sixties forever!

"Mellow out," I told her. "The only thing that's forever is our love for you."

We searched everywhere, but the Time Ball was definitely gone! "You better get to school," Hilda cautioned Sabrina. "Or the man will lay a trip on you."

"Do you guys have to talk like that?" muttered a dour frustrated niece.

"Don't worry," I said, starting to chant. "We'll just fill the house with positive vibes, and the muses will guide us to the Time Ball." After all, what else could we do and not upset the balance of the universe?

"Looking," said Sabrina, impatiently. "Don't forget looking."

In the hallway of Westbridge High School, Sabrina was shocked to find the Time Ball spell in full force. Everyone was dressed in outrageous Sixties' outfits, and didn't seem to think there was anything strange about it. Harvey excitedly told Sabrina and Valerie that he had just bought a 1963 beetle bus. "It only goes thirty-eight miles an hour, but it is so out of sight," he proclaimed.

"Are you going to paint it?" Valerie asked.

"You bet," said Harvey excitedly. "Total psychedelic. Peter Max, to the max."

"You're blowing my mind," cooed Valerie.

"Well, don't make a mess," said Sabrina, heading for class.

She sat at her desk, studying hard, Harvey sitting beside her.

"What's wrong, Sabrina?" he asked. "You seem so uptight."

"I'm just worried about that quiz on 'The Waging of War'," she said.

Suddenly, Harvey raised his fist to the other students.

"Stop the war!" he yelled. The other students chanted back. "Stop the war!"

Mr Kraft entered. He was dressed as a hippie, and had long hair. He gave the peace sign to the class as the chanting rang out.

"Absolutely. Right on," he agreed. "Power to the people."

Sabrina raised her hand. "I have a question about the quiz today."

Mr Kraft looked offended. "Quiz? A quiz only tests what you`ve been told, not who you are."

He pulled a guitar from behind his desk and started strumming it, singing `Kum-ba-ya`. The whole class held hands, and joined in.

"Let`s take it into the hall!" cried Mr Kraft, leading the class, everyone still singing.

"Okay, this is weird," laughed Sabrina. "But at least it`s not a test on a fat book."

Lunchtime came and everyone was sitting on the floor of the cafeteria, including Mrs. Quick.

"What`s this?" Sabrina asked Harvey when she arrived.

"A sit-in," he told her.

"Against the war?"

"No, against the lack of vegetarian food on the cafeteria menu," said Harvey.

"We will not eat our animal friends!" cried Mrs Quick with passion.

Harvey handed Sabrina a flower. "Are you in?" he asked. "If you`re not part of the solution, you`re part of the problem." Sabrina had to think for a minute, during which, Harvey started chanting, "No beef!"

"No beef! No beef! No beef!" everyone else joined in.

Sabrina found a seat next to Valerie. Val's heart was all for the cause, but she wasn't so sure about her taste buds. "It`s so exciting, being part of this movement," she said over the noise of the crowd. "And tofu will grow on me, right?"

A cafeteria employee came in with a megaphone, and announced that the school would give in to the demands. Starting the next day, the cafeteria would serve vegetarian meals.

"All right!" cheered Sabrina, getting caught up in the moment. "They actually listened to us." She was starting to like the Sixties!

And then reality set in!

When Sabrina returned to the College Fair, she was told she could no longer apply to Franklin & Lee.

"Franklin & Lee is a mens` college, the recruiter said. Girls aren`t allowed!

"That`s because men rule the world," an angry Mrs Quick said, when Sabrina told her. "And they do it by oppressing women, forcing us into stereotypical roles and shoes that create permanent foot problems. Here. Let`s take off our bras and burn them in defiance of the misogynistic patriarchy."

Sabrina thought better of that! "You know what? I think I have to meet Harvey," she said, hurrying off. "But maybe we can burn our underwear later."

Harvey didn`t see why Sabrina was making a fuss.

"You don`t need a career," he told her. "You`re my lady. We`ll grow our own food, you`ll have my children, and someday, if it`s not too much of a hassle, I might even marry you."

"I`m sorry," said Sabrina, staring in growing disbelief and anger at Harvey. "I stopped listening after `my lady`."

Rushing home, Sabrina demanded that we find that Time Ball! Just then, Salem sauntered downstairs, wearing love beads. Sabrina smelled his breath. Sardines.

"Salem, you ate my Time Ball!" she cried. "All right. Fork it over."

"Yeah, Salem," agreed Hilda. "I`m getting sick of sitting on the floor with my legs crossed."

"What am I supposed to do?" he wailed. "It`s in my stomach."

I knew just what to do.

"This better not involve a rubber glove," groaned Salem. But I had something else in mind. His fur-ball medicine! It was the only way to get that Time Ball and get back to our normal time.

But, Salem had no intention of taking his medicine. He made a dash for freedom, and this time dived straight through the cat-flap.

"Ha! Your evil plan backfired!" he laughed, disappearing. "I`m skinny enough to get through my cat door. You`ll never catch me now!"

"Oh, no," groaned Sabrina. "Now what do we do?"

"Get a dog?" suggested Hilda.

Salem ran all the way to the highway and hitched a ride in a van driven by hippies.

"Hey, a hitch-hiking cat. Far out," said the driver to his companions. "Let`s take him to San Francisco with us."

"Righteous," said Salem, much to the hippies surprise. "Let`s motor."

"Did this cat talk?" gasped the driver. "Or am I picking up his thoughts telepathically?"

"You`re right," said Salem, settling down. "You can read my mind. And now you`re sensing my great need to stop in Philadelphia for a cheese-steak."

The driver was blown away. "I`m communicating with animals! This is so radical."

"Just drive, Woodstock boy," chuckled Salem, as the van drove off into the setting sun.

But don`t worry - we soon got that pesky cat, the Time Ball and our lives back again.

Swingin' Sixties!

Peace, sisters! Mellow out! Feel the vibes! Right on! And while you`re doing that, tell the times listed below and discover six words associated with the Swingin` Sixties! Groovy! Power to the People! (And don`t forget us cats!)

STOCK

ICAL

TIES

HIP

EDELIC

WOOD

OUT

SIX

RAD

PSYCH

FAR

PIES

A - Five minutes past eight

B - Twenty five minutes to two

C - Twenty five minutes past three

D - Twenty minutes past eleven

E - Ten minutes to six

F - Quarter to twelve

Sabrina Goes To Rome

Original story written by Daniel Berendsen

My globe-trotting adventure to Rome, that totally cool `Eternal City`, kicked off when I received a family heirloom, a beautiful antique gold locket, from my dad.

The locket had been sealed for almost four hundred years. In two weeks, the magic trapped inside it would be lost forever unless someone could find a way to open it. Through the centuries, everyone else in the family had tried and failed. Now it was my turn!

Dad`s note finished by saying, "The secret to the locket lies in Rome. Have a wonderful time…and remember to let the magic guide you."

So, here I was, at a charming Roman pensione, run by the cheerful Signora Guadagno and her cute eighteen year old son, Alberto. I was ready for two, fun-filled, mystery-solving, cat-free weeks, until I found Salem stowed away in my backpack. Well, two out of three isn't bad.

I was sharing a room with Gwen, a British girl who was my age. And guess what? It turned out that Gwen was also a witch! (Only she wasn`t very good!)

Signora Guadagno's family had lost their magic a long time ago, which is why she was happy to open her home to young witches every now and then. And, that's how she knew all about my locket – and why it wouldn't open. "Sophia di Borgheses. She was a beautiful witch," the Signora nodded. "From a powerful family. She fell in love with a mortal. An artist, Roberto Raoli, and he couldn`t be trusted."

It seemed that Sophia foolishly told this Roberto that she was a witch. And if a mortal betrays your secret to others, you are stripped of your powers and cast out!

The next morning, Gwen and Alberto, (who Gwen had a big crush on!), accompanied me through the crowded streets as I attempted to figure out a way to open the locket.

We stopped to admire the beautiful Trevi Fountain. Tossing in a coin, I made a wish. Then I tried again to open the locket. No luck. It wasn`t going to be that easy. I stared at my reflection in the water. It was dressed like a Sixteenth century noblewoman!

Freaked, I leapt back, colliding with a young - and very cute! - American photographer who sold pictures to tacky tabloids. His name was Paul and I ran into him again later that day, in the Statue Gallery of the Museo Nazionale Romano, a very famous Roman museum. They had some antique jewellery very similar to Sophia`s locket and I was hoping to find some answers to my quest. Paul was with his friend, Max.

I'd lost Gwen at the famous statue of David. That was probably a good thing, since she kept trying her magic, and it usually went terribly wrong. This time she managed to accidentally bring David to life.

Completely flipped out by what she had done, she hunted me down and dragged me away from Paul. I didn't want to leave, but how was I going to explain the half-naked man with the slingshot wandering the museum?

"All I did," she explained.

"Was…"

Gwen pointed her finger. POOF! A flash of magic, and a row of marble statues came alive! Staying calm, I quickly zapped them - and David - back to their natural state again.

"Come on," I said. "Let`s get out of here."

What I didn`t realise was that Paul and Max had seen the whole thing. They quickly came to the only obvious conclusion…that I was a witch!

The following morning, I looked out my bedroom window to find Paul in the street below, sitting on his scooter, holding a single flower up towards me.

I know I was in Rome to solve the mystery of the locket, but… Then, I had an idea.

"My father`s note said to follow the magic," I told Gwen, excitedly. "And he was there when I saw that reflection…" I knew I could make it all work!

and Alberto there so that we could check the Hall of Records for information on Sophia. Paul asked me to meet him again the following day at the flower market. As if I was going to miss that date!

In the Reading Room of City Hall or the Palazzo Senatorio as it was called (don't you just love how everything sounds in Italian?!), Gwen discovered an entry for Sophia in a huge, old census book. Alberto translated it for us and it turned out to include her address...and the street was still there!

Gwen and I took off on Alberto's scooter to find Sophia's old house. Paul and Max and their video camera hid out, and then followed us as closely as they could without being detected..

"Don't lose 'em," Max shouted, as Paul revved up his scooter.

I didn't know the city, and Gwen apparently didn't know how to read a map, so we needed directions to Sophia's house - rapidamente. I pointed at the scooter and told it to take us to the address.

The scooter TOOTED twice and sped off, madly weaving in and out of people and traffic. We turned into a dead-end street, heading straight for a brick wall! Waah!

Zapping the wall, I made it disappear. Phew! We flew out of the other side, barely staying on the scooter!

Behind us, Paul was forced to skid his scooter as the wall re-materialised before them! Max fell off, landing on boxes of rotting fruit.

"Okay," he gasped. "That we should have gotten on tape."

Very soon, Gwen and I were inside Sophia's once elegant house. It now looked sad, covered in dust and cobwebs. Upstairs, in what was once the

We went for breakfast at a small street café along the Piazza Di Spagne, near the famous Spanish Steps. He seemed so sweet, and I was really starting to like him.

What I didn't know was, that it was all a ploy by Paul and Max to trick me into doing magic. They planned to get it all on tape to sell to a sleazy Italian publisher for a hundred thousand dollars.

Later, Paul dropped me at the historic Piazza Del Campidoglio, I was meeting up with Gwen ballroom, I did a few spins in front of the mirrors lining the walls. And jumped in fright!

Instead of my reflection, it was the reflection from the Trevi fountain, with me dressed as a sixteenth century noblewoman. It was as if Sophia was trying to tell me something!

I could hear dad`s voice in my head: "Let the magic guide you."

Getting an idea, I ran my hand along the dusty mantelpiece. Then I pointed my finger at the dust on my hand and spoke a magic incantation.

"Soot and grime, dust of time, take us back, to the scene of the crime."

Suddenly, there were sounds of a party. Classical music was playing. And here and there were shimmering, translucent guests. It was impossible to make out the faces, they were completely see-through - the ghosts of a party past!

And on the far wall, I saw a portrait of a woman. It was shimmering too brightly to make out any detail. But I knew.

"It`s a portrait of Sophia," I told a startled Gwen. "That`s what she wanted me to see."

The painting had to be in Rome somewhere. I was sure it was a clue to the spell needed to open the locket. We just needed to find it!

But not until we had had some fun! Next day, we all met Paul at the flower market.

As usual, he was the perfect date. Gwen tried to get Alberto to be a perfect date too, without much success. So, moving behind a flower stall, she put a spell on him.

"Alberto who with my heart does play, fly to my side on wings of grey," she said, pointing at him as he walked with me and Paul. "And there you`ll stay without delay."

Much to Gwen`s surprise and delight, Alberto disappeared from beside me...but then she realised he wasn`t standing next to her, either!

"Alberto?" she said hesitantly, peeking around the side of the stall. But the only thing she found there was a pigeon. When Gwen almost stepped on the bird, it flapped up into her face and Gwen angrily shooed it away.

As for Alberto, he was nowhere to be seen!

It was only that evening, when Signora Guadagno was getting concerned that she hadn`t seen Alberto all day, that Gwen told me word for word the spell she had cast.

"Good news, he`s still in Rome," I told her. "Bad news, he`s a pigeon."

Luckily, there was a reversing spell and it was fairly simple. Gwen had to kiss Alberto. This delighted Gwen since that had been her intent all along.

"Not Alberto the boy," I explained. "Alberto the pigeon."

"Figures, my first kiss, and it`s with a pigeon," she groaned.

The next week we searched the libraries trying to find Sophia`s portrait, visited the wonderful tourist attractions and kissed all of the pigeons along the way. Gwen joined Paul and me for the fun stuff, but she was on her own with the pigeons. We checked out the Colloseum, the Pantheon and, the Roman Forum. Rome is a fabulous city, especially when your tour guide is as cute and funny as Paul.

Throughout our travels, Max, was secretly following us, waiting for me to perform some magic that he could capture on film. When I wouldn't cooperate, he just got more and more frustrated. Especially since his friend seemed to be having so much fun.

We had spent so much time together that Paul realized something was troubling me. He asked me to trust him, and I wanted to. So I explained that I was trying to find Sophia's portrait. Apparently working for a sleazy tabloid has it's perks. Paul used their research department and tracked down the painting!

Next day, in the portrait room of the Capitoline Museum, Paul, Gwen, Max and I gathered around a large painting of Sophia. I felt like I could have been looking in a mirror. We were almost identical...except that Sophia looked unbearably sad.

Heading home through the Piazza Navone, I told Gwen what was troubling me about the painting.

"She looked trapped," I said.

"Maybe she just found out that Roberto betrayed her," suggested Gwen.

Salem was more concerned that I had told Paul about Sophia and the locket.
"Why?" I asked. "Paul's a great guy. Besides, it's not like he has any clue I'm a witch." If only I had known!

Sitting at a little outdoor café, Gwen thought she saw Alberto amongst a flock of pigeons in the square. While she dragged me on a wild goose - sorry, pigeon - chase, Paul and Max discussed their plan to expose me to the world.

"This chick is leaving in three days and we don't have anything," Max grumbled.

Paul was finding it a lot harder than he thought it would be.

"Pretending to like her, or getting her to do a little magic for the camera?" growled Max,

unaware that Alberto the pigeon had landed on the back of a chair, and was listening in on the conversation.

"Who says I'm pretending?" demanded Paul.

"Well, I hope you are because she's not going to be too fond of you when she finds out you were scammin' her to make a bundle. So, are we still going to do this?"

Paul sighed. "Yeah, we're still doin' it."
Alberto was furious. Somehow, he had to warn me!

Later, as we crossed the bridge at Pont Sant'Angelo, I asked Paul why he had chosen to live in Rome.
"I was adopted when I was about two by this great couple,"

Across the dance floor I could see Sophia. She looked so radiant and happy, dancing with Roberto Raoli - the handsome young artist who was about to betray her!

Sophia was still wearing the locket – which explained why I didn't have it. At first she was alarmed to see someone who looked just like her, but was then delighted when I pulled her aside and told her I was a distant relative - like, four hundred years distant!

Since I had come from the future, she wanted me to tell her family how happy she and Roberto would be, so they would know it was all right for her to marry a mortal!

Of course, I couldn't interfere with history, so I couldn't say anything to her parents. Then, Sophia showed me the guy her family wanted her to marry. His name was Lorenzo, a creepy, swarthy looking guy.

"But I have to trust what my heart is telling me," Sophia said. Can't argue with that!

Sophia had already told Roberto that she was a witch, so she believed that since he hadn't betrayed her yet, he never would. And she wanted me to tell that to her family. Yeah, right.

While Sophia went to bring her family over to meet me, I saw Lorenzo handing over money to another man, who I later discovered was Roberto's best friend, Mercutio. What was going on?!

I knew I was going to wind up interfering, changing history and causing more trouble than Salem on his worst day if I didn't get out of there and fast. Then I remembered that I hadn't asked Sophia how to open the locket. I did a quick about-face and bumped straight into Roberto.

"A pleasure," he said pretty suavely, I've gotta admit. "Have we met?"

"You don't think I'm Sophia?" I asked. Everyone else so far had mistaken me for my long, lost cousin.

"I have spent the last year staring into her eyes as I painted this picture," he said, showing me the portrait of Sophia behind me. "You are not my Sophia."

To my surprise, this was not the painting in the museum. In this one, Sophia was smiling!

he explained. "But when they died a couple of years ago I found out I'm not Irish like I always thought growing up. I'm Italian. So when I take my pictures I think maybe one of those old guys is my grandfather. Maybe that woman over there is my sister. I guess I'm just searching for a past."

Like me with Sophia, I thought.

Next morning, accompanied by Gwen and Salem, I returned to the museum, determined to ask Sophia how to open my locket. Much to their misgivings, I magically jumped into the painting and disappeared!

I found myself in the ballroom of Sophia's house, back in the year 1598. Once again there was a party going on (these people sure did have a lot of parties!), and the ballroom was beautiful. Music was playing. Dozens of elegant guests were dancing.

I was now magically dressed in the costume of the time ,and I looked just like I had in my reflection in the fountain. But my locket was missing.

Excusing himself, Roberto went over to speak to Mercutio. I spotted Sophia looking for me, so I ducked into an alcove, where I overheard Roberto's conversation with his friend. Discussion soon turned to arguing. Mercutio was telling an angry Roberto that he couldn't marry Sophia because strange, unexplainable things always happened around her.

Desperate for Mercutio to understand, Roberto made him promise not to tell anyone what he was about to reveal.

"Don't say it," I groaned. "Please don't say it."

"Sophia's a witch," said Roberto.

He said it!

Unfortunately, Sophia had overheard the conversation too.

"How could you betray me?" she wailed, after a shocked Roberto had chased her upstairs into the drawing room where Lorenzo and her family were waiting .

"I didn't mean to," explained a tortured Roberto. "He was worried about me…Sophia, you have to forgive me."

"Unfortunately, it's not up to her to forgive," Lorenzo snarled. "Sophia knew the consequences of telling you her secret." He glared at Sophia. "As is the custom, you will stripped of your powers and cast out."

"No. Please," cried Sophia. "Another chance?"

Lorenzo smirked. "Maybe if you begged for your family's mercy they might let you keep your powers, if…you'd agree to marry me, and never see this pathetic mortal soul again."

Oooh! Sleazoid or what? But I wasn't going to let him get away with it!

"Roberto didn't mean to tell," I told Sophia. "He was tricked. He really loves you." I pointed to Mercutio. "Lorenzo paid that guy

a lot of money to get Roberto to say it."

Sophia was horrified. She realised that her own family was behind the betrayal!

"You'd rather I honoured my magic before my heart," she cried, wrenching off her locket and opening it. "If my power is what you want, then my power you shall have." All her magic power swirled out of her finger and flew into the locket. "I will follow my heart."

Sophia threw the locket at Lorenzo, who immediately tried to open it, but it was sealed tight.

"The locket can only be opened by someone who understands and truly believes," Sophia finished, before rushing off with Roberto.

Lorenzo ordered his guards to stop them, but I zapped a heavy tapestry down on them. THUMP!

Roberto threw me a sword. "You might need it," he said, before disappearing forever with his one true love.

"En garde!" I cried, charging into battle against the guards like some swash-buckling adventurer. Sword fighting in a ball gown definitely puts you at a disadvantage, so I quickly zapped up some more appropriate apparel. Now, we had a fair fight!

Twelve years of gymnastics finally paid off as I back-flipped over the side of the banister and landed beside the portrait. This was where I came in. I pointed and the portrait crashed down on top of me!

When the guards lifted it up…I had vanished! Woo Hoo!

Furious, Lorenzo zapped the portrait with his magic. Sophia`s smile turned into a frown.

That evening, back in our room at Signora Guadagno`s house, I still couldn`t open the stupid locket!

"At least you were able to help Sophia and Roberto be together," said Gwen.

"Sometimes it`s so hard to date a mortal," I sighed, thinking of Paul. "There`s a part of you that you can`t share."

Signora Guadagno came in, still wondering where Alberto was. "I have not seen him in days," she grumbled. "Up early, in late."

"Ah, you know Alberto," I said, as a pigeon landed on the window sill. "He`s always flying off somewhere."

Paul was home, getting ready for his last date with me. I was leaving the next day, and they still didn't have any of my magic on tape. Max wasn't too thrilled about that, but Paul was starting to feel guilty. Guess he liked me as much as I'd grown to like him.

"I feel like I can tell her anything," he said. "But I know I`m lying to her the whole time."

He decided there and then to tell me the truth!

Max was furious. It would blow their whole scheme to get rich quick.

"Fine. Handle it your way," he snapped, as Paul left to meet me. Max picked up his video camera, grinning to himself. "And I`ll handle it mine."

After I had left the house, Gwen noticed the pigeon still on the window sill. Giving it once last chance, she lifted it up and kissed it. POOF! it changed back into Alberto!

"I`m me again!" he cheered, giving Gwen a kiss. Then he remembered what he had overheard Max and Paul discussing.

"If Sabrina tells Paul she`s a witch," groans Gwen. "She`ll never be able to take it back. We have to warn her."

She pointed a finger. POOF! Gwen and Alberto disappeared.

Figuring whatever Gwen had tried, had failed Salem sighed and leapt onto the open windowsill. "If you want something done right…"

Meeting Paul at the Trevi fountain, I stared into the water, catching a glimpse of Sophia.

"You want to make a wish?" Paul asked me, offering me a coin and then tossing in one himself. "Sabrina, there`s something I want to tell you…"

Knowing what he had wished for since moving to Rome I decided to make it come true. "Come on,"I said, pulling him onto the fountain next to me. I pointed, and we disappeared into the fountain with a magical SPLASH!

We found ourselves in a beautiful field of the Italian countryside, overlooking a valley.

Paul was shocked. "How did we get here?"

"Paul, I`m a witch," I said, revealing all. "Fulfilling wishes is just a perk of the job. We`re about twenty minutes outside of Rome…if you drive, that is."

He didn`t understand. This wasn`t his wish.

"This isn`t," I smiled. "But they are."

I pointed to an old farmhouse on the edge of the field. A large Italian family was having dinner outside under a tree.

Paul gasped. "My family?"

"I think your grandfather is the big guy at the end of the table."

"Sabrina, thank you," he said, pulling me into his arms and kissing me.

And with that we magically burst back out into the Trevi fountain!

"There`s one little thing," I told him, "You can never tell anyone I`m a witch."

Paul promised. He would never

tell another soul.

Hidden behind a statue, Max had caught everything on tape!

Salem ran up to us and jumped onto Paul's back. Gwen and Alberto then suddenly appeared too. They had gotten a little lost, ending up in Greenland!

"Sabrina, he set you up," hissed Salem. I grabbed the anxious cat off of my new boyfriend. "What are you talking about?"

"He and Max are writing an exposé on you and selling it," chimed in Gwen.

I was totally freaked out at Paul. "You already knew I was a witch and you didn`t say anything? I can`t believe I trusted you."

Angrily pushing him away, I disappeared into the night.

"You`ve got to believe me," Paul pleaded to my friends. "I never wanted to hurt her."

A furious Gwen decided to pay him back. She pointed a finger at him, planning on turning him into a rabbit…or a chicken.

But her magic backfired again. She turned poor Alberto into a goat!

While a distraught Gwen led Alberto away, Max ran up to Paul, video camera in hand. "That was incredible. I got everything. In the fountain, out of the fountain, talking cat, goat boy. We are going to be so rich."

"Shut up, Max!" yelled Paul, angrily pushing him into the fountain. SPLOOSH!

Back in my room, totally disillusioned, I was using magic to pack my suitcase. I had already turned Alberto back into a boy, but I let him think Gwen did it. He asked Gwen if she would go out with him! "I got my wish," sighed Gwen, dreamily. Opening a window, I looked sadly out over the rooftops.

"But who`s going to make mine come true?" I said.

Early the next morning, a taxi picked up me and Salem. Saying my goodbyes to everyone, I headed off to the airport, hoping in my heart that I might see Paul, once last time. No luck.

But as we passed the Trevi fountain, I knew one last thing I had to do. There was one last person I had to say good-bye to.

"I`m sorry I couldn`t open the locket," I told Sophia, standing in front of her portrait in the museum, still wearing the locket around my neck. "I thought by following my heart like you did, that would be the answer. But I was wrong."

"No you weren`t, Sabrina." It was Paul. He knew that I'd come to say good-bye to Sophia. "Your heart didn`t lie to you. I did."

He dumped a mangled mess of video tape on the bench in front of me.

"One wish fulfilled," he said.

I smiled. "I was right," I said, hugging him.

The locket began to glow. Slowly opening, Sophia`s magic swirled out and circled around us before shooting into the painting. Sophia was smiling again, exactly the way Roberto had painted her!

On one side of the locket was a picture of Sophia and Roberto. On the other, an inscription in Italian: `Aveti confidenza al vostro cuore`.

Paul translated for me. "Trust you heart."

"I always do," I said, smiling up at Sophia.

Exiting the museum, hand-in-hand, Paul turned to me, looking worried.

"What about Max?" he gasped. "I`ll never tell anyone and I destroyed the tape, but…"

"You won`t have to worry about Max," I laughed. "Gwen isn`t the greatest witch, but she taught me a spell or two. Now if I could just remember…"

I pointed.

"No, that`s not it."

I pointed again. "Nope, wrong again." I giggled. "I hope Max is enjoying this as much as I am."

In the apartment, Max stood in the middle of the room, a terrified expression on his face. POOF! He turned into a cow. POOF! He turned into a llama. POOF! A warthog!

"Wait a minute," I said. "That`s not it, either…"

I knew Max would never tell anyone I was a witch!

True Or False?

Sabrina certainly had some fun on her trip to Rome - a bit too much fun, if you ask me! (Just who is this Paul guy, anyway?!) Take this cool True or False quiz to see how much of Sabrina`s adventure you can remember. You`ll be awarded three `spells` for each statement you get right - see how many spells you can collect! (And no cheating by referring back to the story!)

1 - Rome is known as the Internal City. **T** **F**

2 - Sabrina shared a room with a witch called Gwen. **T** **F**

3 - Gwen first turned poor Alberto into a parrot. **T** **F**

4 - The Piazza del Campidoglio is where the Hall of CDs is kept. **T** **F**

5 - The Trevi Fountain was so-called because of the fountain pens thrown in the water.

□ T □ F

6 - Roberto Raoli was an artist.

□ T □ F

7 - A portrait of Sophia was discovered in the Capitoline Museum.

□ T □ F

8 - The Piazza di Spaghetti was near the Spanish Steps.

□ T □ F

9 - Paul and Mark planned to expose Sabrina as a witch.

□ T □ F

10 - The Pont sant Angelo is a river with a bridge over it.

□ T □ F

11 - Trying to reach Sabrina to warn her, Gwen and Alberto ended up in Iceland.

□ T □ F

12 - Roberto threw Sabrina a rolling pin to fight off the guards trying to catch them.

□ T □ F

13 - Sabrina went back in time to the year 1489 to find Sophia.

□ T □ F

14 - Gwen`s first kiss was with a pigeon!

□ T □ F

15 - "Averti confidenza al vostro cuora" means "trust your heart".

□ T □ F

When In Rome...

Hi everyone! I had a fantastic time in Rome! If you ever have an opportunity to visit this magical city, then do so - it really will put a `spell` on you!

While I was there, I came up with this cool word search! Can you find the listed names in this grid? They might be horizontal, vertical, diagonal - or even back-to-front! (Hey, I`m not going to make it too easy!) There is one name that is NOT in the grid at all, and one name that is listed TWICE! Good luck!

ALBERTO
ETERNAL CITY
GWEN
LOCKET
LORENZO
MUESO NAZIONALE
PENSIONE
PIAZZA NAVONE
PIGEON
PORTRAIT
ROBERTO RAOLI
ROMAN FORUM
ROME
SABRINA
SCOOTER
SOPHIA
TREVI FOUNTAIN

P	I	A	Z	Z	A	N	A	V	O	N	E
O	B	M	U	G	L	I	S	R	B	A	L
R	E	C	W	S	F	A	J	E	T	E	A
T	O	E	K	A	L	T	R	N	M	M	N
R	N	M	S	B	T	N	V	O	P	U	O
A	T	Q	E	R	A	U	R	I	K	R	I
I	F	R	G	I	K	O	L	S	J	O	Z
T	T	Z	H	N	T	F	I	N	P	F	A
O	W	P	B	A	P	I	G	E	O	N	N
D	O	U	E	M	C	V	A	P	L	A	O
S	S	C	O	O	T	E	R	Z	D	M	S
C	U	O	Z	N	E	R	O	L	V	O	E
O	L	O	C	K	E	T	P	T	D	R	U
Y	T	I	C	L	A	N	R	E	T	E	M

Sabrina And The Beanstalk

Original story written by Carrie Honigblum & Renee Phillips

Hilda here! Zelda has already told you about one of Sabrina`s adventures. Now it`s my turn! (Trust me, mine`s better!)

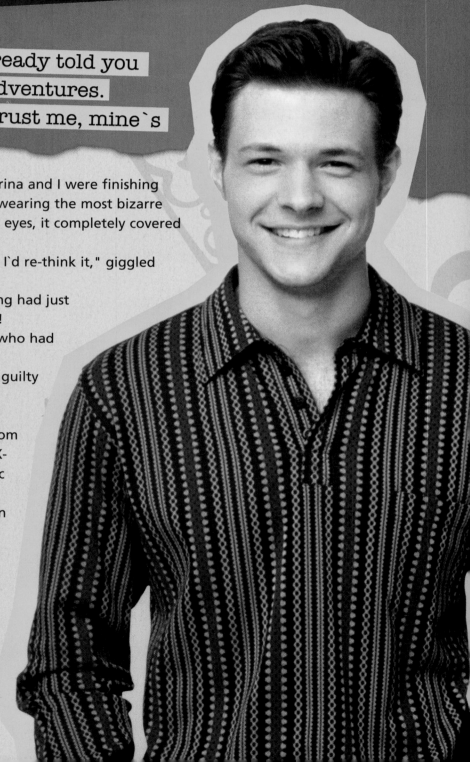

One bright Spring morning, as Sabrina and I were finishing breakfast in the kitchen, Zelda came in, wearing the most bizarre helmet. Brightly decorated with glowing eyes, it completely covered her head!

"If that`s a new fashion statement, I`d re-think it," giggled Sabrina.

But it seems that my scientific sibling had just invented the first portable X-Ray helmet!

Sabrina was more concerned with who had eaten all the contents of the new box of breakfast cereal. Salem tried not to look guilty - and failed miserably!

"Let`s do a cat scan," said Zelda, helping Sabrina to slip on the helmet. From inside the helmet, Sabrina could see an X-Ray image of Salem that showed a plastic toy soldier in his stomach.

"Salem!" she said crossly. "You even ate the prize!

Just then, Harvey arrived at the front door. Quickly doing a witch check, making sure all magic and talking cats were cleared from the living room, she let him in.

"So, what would be a good transportation system for the town of Westbridge?" said Harvey, as they settled on the couch to start working on their school project.

"Hmm," said Sabrina, thinking hard.

Time ticked by. Tick! Tick! Tick!

But instead of studying, they wasted the time having pillow fights, watering the plants and channel-hopping TV shows.

By the time Harvey left, the amount of homework that had actually been done was...a big, fat zero!

"Sabrina," I said, sternly. "You`ve really got to stop procrastinating." Which is pretty funny, coming from me, Queen of the Procrastinators!

"I just wish I could get motivated," sighed Sabrina.

"Magic jumping beans," I suggested, explaining that they would give Sabrina a lot more hop-to.

In the dining room, Sabrina opened Zelda`s lab-top, which contains dozens of magical ingredients. Unfortunately, we didn`t have any that were required to make magic jumping beans.

So Sabrina decided to substitute other ingredients instead. Big mistake! You can`t mess around with magic!

Sabrina mixed her mixed-up ingredients. There was a puff of smoke, and a packet of colourful magic jumping beans appeared.

"Hold some beans in your hand, shake vigorously and you will feel instantly energetic," Sabrina read from the packet. So she grabbed a handful and shook them. Nothing happened. She shook them again. Still nothing.

"Well, these beans are lame!" she said angrily, tossing them into the trash can, which she then took out into the yard. She was supposed to take the trash to the curb, but procrastinating again, she decided to do it the next day!

The next morning, Zelda and I were in the kitchen when there was a tremendous cracking noise and the whole house began violently shaking!

"Earthquaaaake!" Salem cried, looking for cover.

The commotion brought Sabrina in, too. "Is that a beanstalk?" she gasped in amazement.

We all looked outside to find a huge beanstalk in the yard, with giant leaves hanging from it, stretching up into the clouds!

"Did someone throw out magic beans?" asked Zelda, looking accusingly at Sabrina, who had to admit that she had.

"Did you follow the recipe carefully?" asked Zelda.

"Sure," said Sabrina. "With a few substitutions." The trouble was, she couldn't remember what she had put in the recipe.

"I was going to write it down, but..." she said, her words trailing off.

"See, Sabrina?" Zelda sighed. "Procrastination only makes things worse."

Sabrina knew she'd been wrong, but first things first! We had to hide a 300 foot beanstalk! Zelda and I cupped our hands around our mouths and made the sound of a loud fog horn. Suddenly, the whole of Westbridge was blanketed in a thick fog. That should do the trick. Now we just had to consider our options.

We sent Salem, protesting as usual, halfway up the beanstalk to stand guard in case a giant tried to get down. Sabrina suggested we hire a tree trimmer to cut down the beanstalk.

"This is a - beanstalk, Sabrina," I told her. "It's going to take a lot more than tree trimmers."

Just then, Harvey arrived to work on the school project. Seeing Zelda's X-ray helmet, he mistook it for a virtual reality game!

"Sure," laughed Sabrina, relieved he hadn't seen the beanstalk in the yard. "That's a good explanation."

He then noticed the discarded packet of magic jumping beans. Mistaking them for jelly beans, he popped one in his mouth! Next thing you know, he was catapulted out of the back door and hurtled straight up the beanstalk!

Oops!

Using a periscope we keep in the kitchen ceiling (What?? You don't have one?!), we could see a rather surprised and confused Harvey on top of the clouds. He was approaching a quaint cottage with a thatched roof. The door creaked open to

his knocking, and Sabrina was relieved to see it answered by an attractive woman, who smiled at Harvey.

"Oh, good," Sabrina gasped. "It`s not a giant."

"It`s worse," said Zelda, taking a look. "It`s the Wicked Witch! And worst of all, she feasts on mortals."

A horrified Sabrina wanted to go up the

Meantime, the Wicked Witch had invited Harvey into her cottage, encouraging him to eat lots of delicious meals, each one sprinkled with `Fatten Up` to speed his...well, fattening up.
Thinking he had died from eating a bad jelly bean and was now in Heaven, Harvey decided to make the best of it. He began stuffing himself with food, unaware that the Wicked Witch was standing behind him, sharpening a huge meat knife - but Sabrina could see everything!

beanstalk and save Harvey, but we told her the high altitude could knock out her powers - then she would be no match for the Wicked Witch!

Telling Sabrina to keep watch through the periscope, we hurried to the YMCA - the Yikes! Magic Crisis Agency. They specialised in solving these sorts of problems.
But when we arrived there, we were stuck in a long line. How long was it? Well, some witches had been waiting for over fifty years! That`s government bureaucracy for you!

Panicking, she rushed into the yard and started climbing up the beanstalk! Salem, half-way up on his guard post, tried to stop her, but Sabrina was determined.

"I`m going up and don`t try to stop me, cat," she growled, pushing past him. So Salem had no other choice than to follow her, even though he was terrified of heights!

Reaching the clouds far ahead of Salem, Sabrina hurried to the Wicked Witch`s cottage. She needed a plan! Pointing at herself, she changed her clothes into a smart business suit and tie, with her hair up. A sample case appeared beside her.

"There's nothing wrong with my magic," she said, remembering our dire words earlier.

Introducing herself as a salesperson from the Confectionery Construction Company, she told the Wicked Witch that the company specialised in gingerbread siding, the sugary smell which really attracted kids!

"Well, I do love children," she said, allowing Sabrina to enter the cottage. "Especially with a béarnaise sauce." Uggh. Gross!

While the Wicked Witch was busy looking through gingerbread sample catalogues Sabrina had given her, my clever young niece sneaked into the kitchen where she found Harvey, bloated like a blimp balloon, still stuffing himself.

"Sabrina!" he gasped. "Oh, no! You ate a bad bean and died, too. What are the odds of that?"

Sabrina quickly explained that Harvey wasn't dead, but would be soon if they didn't escape. The Wicked Witch was planning to cook him!

Talk about a buzz kill! When the Wicked Witch came into the kitchen to ask Sabrina some questions about candy-cane rain gutters, they slipped past her and headed for the front door.

The Wicked Witch suddenly realised that she was being tricked!

Fe, Fi, Fo, Fum," she said, pointing at the front door. "I smell a half mortal."

A massive padlock appeared on the door! Sabrina and Harvey were trapped!

While Salem still struggled to climb up the beanstalk after Sabrina, she remained a prisoner in the Wicked Witch's living room with a terrified Harvey, a pile of food in front of them.

"Come on, kids, eat up," cackled the

Wicked Witch. "I can only see one chin." Then remembering she had some lady fingers baking, she hurried into the kitchen.

Harvey kept watch for the Wicked Witch's return while Sabrina took her chance to escape. She pointed at the padlock on the front door…but nothing happened!

"It must be the high altitude," she groaned. "My powers are knocked out. Why are my aunts always right?" Because we're older and have more experience, and…we'll get to that later. I'm sure you want to hear the rest of the story now.

So, she and Harvey tried eating through the gingerbread walls instead.

"You pesky little entrées," the Wicked Witch purred, returning from tending to her oven. She pointed at them. "If you keep trying to escape, I'll just have to move up my dinner party."

The next second, Sabrina and Harvey found themselves in a giant soup pot, simmering and being prepared as the main course!

Sabrina had to come up with something - and fast! When the Wicked

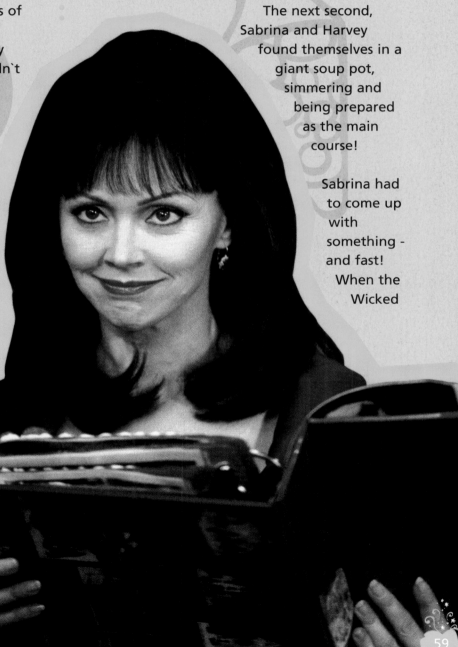

Witch realised she was out of mushrooms and couldn`t make a good gravy without them, Sabrina suggested she keep them simmering for one more day. She`d have time to go get the mushrooms and by then, they`d be a lot more tender, too.

The Witch agreed to put off eating them, and set about looking through the cooking journals she`d been neglecting. The warm kitchen and the reading soon made her doze off!

"I`m beginning to worry," groaned Harvey. "We`re starting to smell good."

Sabrina told him to be quiet as she reached over and gently took hold of the sleeping Wicked Witch`s hand. She pointed the Wicked Witch`s finger at the lock on the front door. A bolt of magic shot out, unlocking the padlock! Then Sabrina turned the Witch`s pointing finger on the pot. Zap! They were free, dry and ready to make a break for it.

Unfortunately, as they ran out of the cottage, Harvey let the door slam shut! The Wicked Witch woke abruptly. She chased after them, waving a rolling pin in her hand! "I don`t like fast food," she complained.

Reaching the beanstalk, they found the Wicked Witch had used her magic to get there first!

"Now I`ve got you," she cackled.

Grabbing hold of the overweight Harvey`s arm, Sabrina swung him into the Wicked Witch, knocking her flying!

Salem appeared at the top of the beanstalk. "Finally!" he gasped, out of breath. "I made it all the way up."

"Go down! Go down!" screamed Sabrina, as she and Harvey started to climb down.

"You`ve gotta be kidding," groaned an exhausted Salem.

But when the Wicked Witch threatened to eat him for dessert, he leapt off the cloud, falling down, down, down through the air! Luckily, being a cat, he landed safely on his feet in the yard!

The climb down sweated all the excess fat off Harvey so that he was back to his normal size.

Looking over Westbridge on the way down, Sabrina thought the town could use a monorail.

"Yeah, we should remember that for our repooo - -" said Harvey, losing his grip! Sabrina instinctively used her magic to save him.

"Hey, my powers are back on," she cheered.

"Get back here, you little lean cuisines!" yelled the Wicked Witch from above them. "Why didn`t I eat you when I had the chance?"

"Because you procrastinated," said Sabrina,

answer from the YMCA. Sabrina had been right, all along! The best thing for a magic beanstalk was a tree trimmer. Go figure!

The tree trimmer quickly cut through the beanstalk…and it disappeared straight into the ground!

"Cool," said Sabrina.

"Yeah, cool," said Harvey, before fainting from all the excitement.

Luckily, when he came to, we had put Zelda`s X-Ray helmet on his head, and he thought he had just been taking part in an exciting - if somewhat bizarre! - virtual reality game!

That evening, Sabrina went to the back door to call Salem for dinner. It wasn`t like him to be late.

"I can`t move," sobbed Salem from somewhere outside. Sabrina looked down and saw the Wicked Witch`s jar of `Fatten Up`. It must have fallen off the beanstalk.

pointing her finger upwards. "Take that!"

The Wicked Witch suddenly found herself padlocked inside her cottage, sitting in front of a tossed salad.

"Oh, no!" she screamed, horrified. "She`s turned me into a vegetarian!"

Sabrina and Harvey reached the bottom of the beanstalk just as we arrived back with a handsome, muscular man carrying a chain-saw. After hours of waiting in line, we finally got an

"Oh, Salem," giggled Sabrina. "You didn`t?"

Salem waddled into sight. He was as big and fat as a black furry medicine ball.

"I did!" he groaned. "Don`t just stand there. Somebody get me a diet soda."

That`ll teach him!

Beanstalk

Sabrina and Harvey need help - fast! Which path should they take down the beanstalk maze to get back to Sabrina`s house and escape the Wicked Witch?

Answer: Path C leads back to Sabrina's house!

Maze-Ness!

Original story written by Sheldon Bull

Pancake Madness

Ever had such a bad craving for something, you just couldn`t resist? I did once...pancakes!

One morning, as Salem and I sat down to breakfast, I realised that we had never had pancakes in our house. So I pointed to the table and two plates stacked with pancakes appeared, oozing with thick syrup. Mmmm-mmmm!

Just as I was about to taste my first mouthful, Aunt Zelda rushed into the kitchen and snatched the fork away from me!

"No pancakes," said Aunt Hilda, joining her. She took my plate and dumped it in the trash.

"Not in this house. Not ever."

Aunt Zelda then explained a frightening Spellman secret. "All Spellmans` have a terrible weakness for pancakes. If you eat even one bite, you won`t be able to stop."

What was the big deal? I could quit at any time. Salem, seemed to be the one with the problem. He hadn't come up for air since he started eating. How come they weren't stopping him?

"Salem's not affected because he's not family," Aunt Zelda explained, deadly serious.

Ahh, so he was just being his usual piggy self. But I was half-mortal. Maybe this weird craving wouldn't affect me!

"We can't take the risk," said Aunt Zelda, putting a spell on me so that I could never again conjure pancake batter.

This was ridiculous! Whoever heard of being addicted to pancakes?!

Waiting until my aunts had left the kitchen, I took a bite of one of Salem's pancakes!

"There, I ate pancakes," I said, grabbing my book bag and heading for school. "And I don't feel one bit addicted. I knew my aunts were over-reacting."

Why don't I ever listen to them?!

The craving for all-things pancakes kicked in at school when I spotted Harvey eating from a carton filled with miniature pancakes.

"Can I have one?" I pleaded.

Normally Harvey would have agreed, but his mom was pregnant and not in the mood to cook, so this was the only hot breakfast he had had all week.

"Come on," I pleaded with him, desperately. "Just one little bite."

"Since when did you become such a pancake fiend?" asked Harvey, finishing off the last pancake before throwing the carton into a trash can and heading off to class.

Making sure no one was looking, I reached inside the trash and pulled out the carton, quickly rubbing my fingers around the greasy interior. Then I slowly sucked the pancake crumbs off them, one by one. Ohh, Heaven!

"My aunts did this to me," I muttered to myself, hurrying off. "They put weird thoughts in my head. I am not getting hooked on pancakes."

But If I thought I had problems, Aunt Hilda`s were even worse!

For some reason the linen closet wouldn`t transport her to the Other Realm. An invisible barrier was stopping her from getting through. It was only when a man from the Witch Immigration service and a cop on a motorbike appeared in the living room that all was revealed.

It seemed that even though Aunt Hilda had been living in the Mortal Realm for two hundred years, she had never actually filled out the proper paperwork. She was, in fact, an illegal immigrant!

The Witch Immigration guy ordered the cop to arrest her, and they headed towards the linen closet. Aunt Zelda demanded to know where they were taking her.

"Back to the Northern sector of the Other Realm where she came from," she was told. Brrr! Now that is a cold place to live!

Back at school, I was feeling a little jittery. Sitting next to Harvey, I took his hand in mine, pulling it towards me as if to kiss it.

"Please stop trying to lick my hands," Harvey snapped. "There`s no syrup on them."

Our teacher, Mrs Quick, was asking the class if anyone had any ideas to raise money for the upcoming school prom. But all I could think of was...

"Pancakes!" I yelled out loudly. Luckily, Mrs Quick thought I meant holding a pancake breakfast at school to raise money.

Mrs Quick thought it was a charming idea. The next morning we would be holding a pancake breakfast. I didn't know whether to be thrilled or panicked.

After school ended, I rushed home, and searched through the kitchen in a mad attempt to find something that tasted like pancakes!

Aunt Zelda was in the living room, talking to Aunt Hilda on the phone. Aunt Hilda was stuck in a run-down bar in the Northern Section of the Other Realm. It was full of mountain men, who spent all their time fighting with each other!

Aunt Zelda promised she`d find a way to get Aunt Hilda back home! "Don`t worry," she said, listening to tables and bottles being smashed in the background. "I`ll think of something."

Spending the evening filling in the immigration forms that Aunt Hilda should have filed two hundred years ago, Aunt Zelda didn`t notice how jittery I was becoming.

It got so bad that, halfway through the night, I was still wide awake, imagining the mouth-watering delight of soft, velvety pancakes melting on my tongue!

Salem caught me downstairs in the kitchen, extremely agitated, trying to make pancakes the old-fashioned mortal way.

"You`re making pancakes, aren`t you?" he hissed accusingly. "You`re hooked! You`re a flapjack fiend!"

I had to admit that I was. And I was worried about the pancake breakfast at school later that morning. Everybody would know my shameful secret. I needed help - fast!

Salem came through for me. Using Aunt Zelda`s lab-top and a recipe from the magic book, we concocted a syrup that would make me hate the taste of pancakes. All I had to do was pour it on before I took the first bite…! Yesss!!

When we got there, the Westbridge High School cafeteria was full of hungry students. And pancakes. There were plates of pancakes stacked up everywhere! Not that I was worried…I had my magic syrup to save me. And then, I didn't! Remembering my craving from yesterday, Harvey had gotten me an extra big stack of pancakes – he's so sweet, isn't he? sigh - and I put my magic syrup bottle down for just a second. I swear.

Next thing I knew, "My syrup! Where`s my syrup?" I squealed, realising that the bottle was gone. The lunch-lady had collected all of the syrup on a tray – including my magical version. And before I could stop them, the other students had all grabbed the bottles, any one of which could have be mine!

"I`ve gotta get out of here," I groaned, feeling the pancake cravings swelling up inside me.

Rushing for the door, I overheard my arch-enemy Libby Chessler talking to a friend.

"Ew, these taste awful," she complained, dropping a syrup-covered pancake back on her plate. My syrup!

"Just one bite," I said, snatching up Libby`s fork and popping some pancake into my mouth.

"Hey, these don't taste awful," I said, feeling the rich, seductive pleasure of pancake melting on my tongue. "They're delicious."

"They're blueberry," snorted Libby. "I don't like blueberry."

Uh-oh. That wasn't my syrup! Which meant...

"Oh, no!" I groaned, the overwhelming addiction for pancakes hitting on me again. "More! I've got to have more!"

I grabbed all the pancakes from Libby's plate, and stuffed them into my mouth. Then I attacked everybody else's pancakes!

"What are you all just standing there for," I screeched. "I need pancakes!"

Just then, a cafeteria worker appeared with a cart loaded with fresh pancakes! I swooped down on them, eating, eating, eating...!!!

And looked up to see everyone staring open-mouthed at me.

Smiling weakly, I wiped the syrup from my mouth. "I hope nobody noticed that."

Aunt Zelda sent off Aunt Hilda's emergency request for a change in immigration status to the Other Realm. Moments later, the toaster pinged and an envelope popped up. Talk about service!

Aunt Hilda could expect a response to her application in...five to ten years?! Talk about your bureaucratic red tape.

But I had big problems of my own. Literally. My body had swollen to the size of a blimp! I called to Aunt Zelda to help me get through the front door.

"I think I'm retaining water," I groaned. "Or syrup."

Aunt Zelda immediately realised what had happened and sent for an Other Realm doctor. He jabbed a magic pin into my side. Ouch!

A hurricane blast of wind almost blew Aunt Zelda, Salem and the doctor off their feet! But when it was over, I was back to my normal size again. Woo-hoo!

Unfortunately, I still wasn't cured of my addiction. Aunt Zelda locked me in my room while I went through pancake detox!

"Just remember," Aunt Zelda said, before leaving to save Aunt Hilda, "It's times like these

that build character."

"I don`t want character," I yelled after her. "I want pancakes."

Oooh! It was agony! Time seemed to go so slowly. And my craving for pancakes seemed to get even worse. I couldn`t stop thinking about them. And when I finally fell into a fitful sleep, what did I dream about? Pancakes! Aaaggghh!!

First I dreamt that Westbridge High was filled with students, singing and dancing, holding plates of delicious, syrup-covered pancakes.

Then I dreamt that Salem had turned into a stack of pancakes!

"Hungry?" the dream Salem asked, before cackling loudly. I ran screaming from him, only to collide with a giant syrup bottle with a woman`s syrup-covered head on top. She introduced herself as Mrs. Mapleton, the syrup dispenser of my dreams!

She took me to the international pancake house. People from all over the world were dressed in their national costume, sitting at tables enjoying plates stacked with pancakes!

"Everyone`s here because they love pancakes, just like you do," Mrs. Mapleton told me.

"But I don`t want to be hooked on pancakes," I groaned. "I forgot about my friends, I forgot about my family. All I could think of was eating pancakes and getting more pancakes." I started to drool at the sight of all those pancakes. "And the butter, and syrup and...maybe I`ll just have one little stack."

This wasn`t going to be as easy as I had hoped!

Meanwhile, in the Northern Sector of the Other Realm, Aunt Zelda had rescued Aunt Hilda from the bar. They were trudging through the deep snow, heading towards the border crossing, the bitter wind howling all around them. Aunt Zelda was planning on smuggling her sister back home if she had to!

A Mountie appeared and said they would have to answer a few standard questions about the Mortal Realm - just to prove they lived there. Aunt Zelda thought it would be easy. After all, she did have three PhDs.

But to her dismay, all the questions were about celebrities! While Aunt Hilda got all the answers right, Aunt Zelda wasn`t able to answer a single question!

"There`s no way you live in the Mortal Realm," said the Mountie, arresting her.

"But I do!" said Aunt Zelda. "I can tell you who wrote `Pride and Prejudice`, who discovered uranium isotope..."

The Mountie interrupted her. "Nobody in the Mortal Realm knows those things," he said. He then dragged her back into the snowy wilderness as Aunt Hilda headed for home!

I was still dreaming I was at the international pancake

house, fighting the urge to succumb to my cravings, but it was so hard. Everybody was telling me to "Eat! Eat! Eat! Eat! Eat!" Noooooo!!!

Then Aunt Hilda shook me awake!

"Is it over?" I gasped.

There was only one way to be sure. In the kitchen, Aunt Hilda conjured up a plate of extra tasty pancakes covered in mouth-watering syrup and butter. She pushed it under my nose. Oh, that smell!

I slammed down the fork I was holding. "No!" I yelled.

"Very good," said Aunt Hilda, relieved. "So how do you feel?"

I felt like I wanted pancakes, but I guess that`s the way I was always going to feel. I`d just have to take one day at a time.

There was a crash of thunder from upstairs. We rushed up to the linen closet to find Aunt

Zelda there, struggling to close the closet door against a powerful Northern Sector blizzard.

It seemed she had been stuck in that awful bar, with the fighting continuing all around her, when she had switched TV to a production of `Swan Lake`.

"The next thing I knew I was being tossed across the border," she explained. And, being the loving aunt that she was, she wanted to know how I was doing?

"I`m just glad I`m not hallucinating, anymore," I chuckled, before seeing Miss Mapleton pass by. "Hi, Mrs. M," I said, waving to her.

And then, realising what I had just seen…I fainted!

"Hard day," said Aunt Zelda, looking down at me.

"Lots of sugar," agreed Aunt Hilda, helping me to bed!

Pancakes Galore!

Did you know that Americans don`t just eat pancakes on Pancake Day - we eat them all year round, especially for breakfast!
(Not too many, though, otherwise we`d become seriously overweight - just ask Sabrina!)

If you would like to make your own pancakes, follow my instructions - and ask a grown-up to help.

You will need

110g plain flour

A pinch of salt

2 large eggs

200ml milk mixed with 75ml water

A little butter for cooking

A sieve and frying pan

Sift the flour and salt into a large bowl, holding the sieve high to give the flour an airing. (Keep the sieve over the bowl or you`ll make a horrible mess!)

Make a well in the centre of the flour and break in the eggs, making sure no shell drops in. Using either a fork or a hand whisk, start to whisk the eggs with the flour.

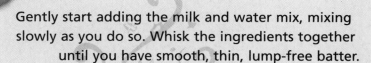

Gently start adding the milk and water mix, mixing slowly as you do so. Whisk the ingredients together until you have smooth, thin, lump-free batter.

Ask a grown-up to melt about a teaspoon of the butter in a frying pan and swirl around. Then pour out the surplus butter. Make sure the pan is really hot. Turn the heat down to medium. Add two tablespoons of batter and swirl it around side to side until the pan is evenly coated. Cook until golden brown underneath.

Use a palate knife to lift the corner of your pancake and turn over. Or ask the grown-up to supervise whilst you toss your pancake. (Not too high!) Pancakes should take about one minute to cook.

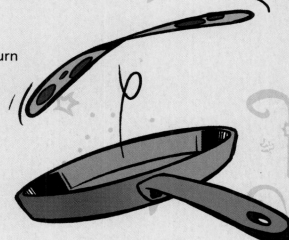

Warm some maple syrup in a saucepan, brush each pancake, roll or fold. Have a jug with warm syrup on the table when serving. You could also make other fillings of your choice, like jam and cream and bananas and cream!

Sabrina Down Under

Original story written by Daniel Berendsen

G`day, Cobbers! Remember Gwen, that wacky British teenage witch, I met on my trip to Rome? Well, we met up again on another vacation - in Australia!

More specifically, the awe-inspiring Great Barrier Reef. Trust me, it is…breathtaking! Two thousand kilometres of stunning clear blue water, magnificent coral formations hundreds of years old and shoals and shoals of brightly-coloured fish. It truly is a paradise on earth!

I`d wanted to visit, ever since I`d read a book called `The Secrets of the Reef` by famed marine biologist Dr. Julian Martin. He had a research institute attached to the resort I was staying at on Hamilton Island.

The island was one of many inside the Reef, beautifully green and ringed with glistening white sandy beaches.

When I arrived by helicopter from the mainland, Gwen was there to greet me. As we hugged I heard two fishermen having an argument.

"I`m telling you, two hours ago my bait can turned into a kangaroo and hopped away," said one.

"Ah, you`re completely daft," snorted the other.

I gave Gwen a withering glare. After all, she had promised me that she wouldn't use magic on this vacation.

"But I`ve been practising," said Gwen, defensively. "I`m really a lot better than the last time you saw me. Watch."
Before I could stop her, she clenched her fist, and the necklaces of shells I had been presented with on my arrival turned into sweet-smelling tropical flowers.

"Wicked," grinned Gwen. "Told you I`ve been practising."

Yeah, it would have been perfect…if she hadn`t also given me a big, fluffy bunny tail!

"In my defence," said Gwen, blushing, as I pointed the tail away, "I didn`t say I was good. I just said I was better."

It didn't really matter. I was in paradise. There were dolphins, fish of every colour of the rainbow and cute guys from every corner of the globe. Best on all? No Salem!

Or, so I thought. At that very moment porters were delivering luggage and a cat case to one of the rooms in my hotel.

"You ever seen this Saberhagen guy?" one of the porters asked the other.

"Nah. No one has," the other porter answered. "And he's been coming here for years."

"What kinda nutcase spends a week locked in a hotel room with a mangy cat?" laughed the first one, sticking his finger through the bars of the case to pet Salem.

He let out a loud yelp as Salem attacked!

"Ow! This thing bit me. I`ll probably need to get a shot."

"And I`ll need to wash my mouth out," hissed Salem, coming out of the case after the porters had left. But then he took in the view from the window. "Hello, paradise."

Salem called the lobby to make sure the manager, knew the drill.

"Of course," the manager said, smarmily. After all, the mysterious Mr Sabenhagen was one of his best customers! "No one is ever to enter your room unannounced. And your cat Salem has complete and total access to the resort. The staff has already been alerted. Your cat`s every whim is our desire."

How the heck had he been swinging that deal all these years without any of us knowing?

Oh well. Back to me! It didn`t take Gwen long to fish out the local talent - she had caught herself a tanned, muscular, handsome guy called Jerome, and introduced him to me as we sat at a beach bar.

"Pleasure, Sabrina," he said, in a very thick Australian accent. "Just tellin` your pommy cobber here that I was afraid there might be too many Steak 'n Kidneys about, but not the case, eh? I`ll pop and get us some lolly water. Hooroo."

As Jerome headed to the bar, Gwen smiled dreamily at me. "Doesn`t he have the cutest accent?"

I grinned. "Can`t understand a word he says. Can you?"

"No," sighed Gwen. "I was hoping you could."

Just then, from down the beach, we heard a loud commotion. A man was raging at two divers who had been looting coral and marine life from the Reef to take home for their collections.

He grabbed their bag, accusing them of being poachers. The divers ran off in embarrassment. Then I realised who the man was - it was Dr. Julian Martin!

around the Reef forever. Then I thought wait a minute...I'm a witch...I don't need to wish! And I turned myself into a fish!

"Scales," I said to a laughing Gwen. "Very in this year."

Sabrina-the-Fish darted off, swimming down, down, through the reef. It was amazing! And so was what I spotted, far deeper than most divers could go - a blue spot butterfly fish. What's the big deal with that? Well, they were supposed to have been extinct for at least fifty years!

Returning to human form, I told Dr. Martin what I had seen. He wasn't sure whether to believe me or not. But what a find it would be if I was right!

Dr. Martin took me to the marine institute to verify my sighting. Our research was interrupted by his assistant who told us that another dolphin had beached in Paradise Cove, on the other side of the island, fungus sores on its body. The doctor speculated some rotten ship had been illegally dumping its waste in the ocean, killing the marine life. Everyone was pretty upset about it, but it was apparently almost impossible to catch the bad guys in the act.

I hurried over to introduce myself. After he had calmed down - he hated people messing with his reef! - I explained how much I had learned about marine life from his book. And how I was now considering becoming a marine biologist.

I must have impressed him, because he invited me to come on a dive he was planning the next day!

Early the next morning, Gwen and I, wearing our diving suits and oxygen masks, swam together around the awesome coral formations, while amazing fish of all shapes and colours darted all around us.

It was so beautiful, I wished I could swim

Meanwhile, Salem wasn't catching much either. He had met a beautiful Persian who just happened to be a witch trapped in the body of a cat. The fact that she was wearing sunglasses and reading a book sort of gave it away!

Her name was Hillary, and Salem was trying to woo her - and failing, big time. She just wasn't interested in him. He even had the hotel manager deliver a bucket of fish to her, but she sent it back.

"I know it's none of my business, sir," the manager told "Mr" Sabenhagen over the phone. "But might I suggest next time you try flowers?"

Poor guy, he didn't know what he was up against!

Later that day, Gwen and I were walking along the beach when we thought we spotted a beached dolphin. Horrified, we hurried over, only to discover it was actually an unconscious, good-looking young man…with a giant fish tail where his legs should have been. Yep, you guessed it. It was a merman!

Desperate to help him, I pointed the three of us back to our bungalow. A maid was cleaning our room, so we picked up the merman and raced out again - and found Salem sitting on a bench, filling out postcards!

Well, that was a surprise! At least we were able to take the merman to Salem's room, and let him recover in a bathtub full of salted water.

Turns out his name was Barnaby, and he lived in Paradise Cove on the other side of the island. A blue fungus was growing on his shoulder. He also had some on his tail.

I remembered Dr. Martin telling me that the beached dolphins were suffering from the same symptoms. If it wasn't treated quickly it could be fatal!

Explaining to a sceptical Barnaby that Gwen and I were witches, I cast a spell and turned his tail into legs. I warned him that the spell would last for forty eight hours and couldn't be reversed. I knew it was kind of an extreme measure, but it was the only way to get him to Dr. Martin for a proper examination.

Turns out, Barnaby didn't mind a bit. "Look at me!" he said in delight, after the spell took effect. "I`m standing!"

"Oh, sure," snorted Salem bitterly. "The fish gets to be a man, but the cat, no."

Heading along the beach to the research institute - Barnaby fascinated by everything he saw - we were spotted by his mermaid sister, Fin, and pet dolphin, Spout. Spout swam to greet us, but Fin stayed in the water, disgusted by Barnaby's new legs. "She`s not the biggest fans of humans," explained Barnaby, after Fin had swum off.

Unknown to us, Barnaby had already been spotted swimming in the sea by Dr. Martin`s assistant, who had taken photographs. The pictures were blurred, and Dr. Martin wasn`t sure if it was someone having a laugh at his expense, but if a merman really was out there, he was determined to find it!

What he didn't know was that the merman found him. So, when I showed him Barnaby`s fungus spots, he was concerned that what was affecting the marine life was now affecting humans too. We left after the doctor gave us some ointment, and he went back to checking the merman photographs. He realised that the size and discolouration on his shoulder was identical to the one on

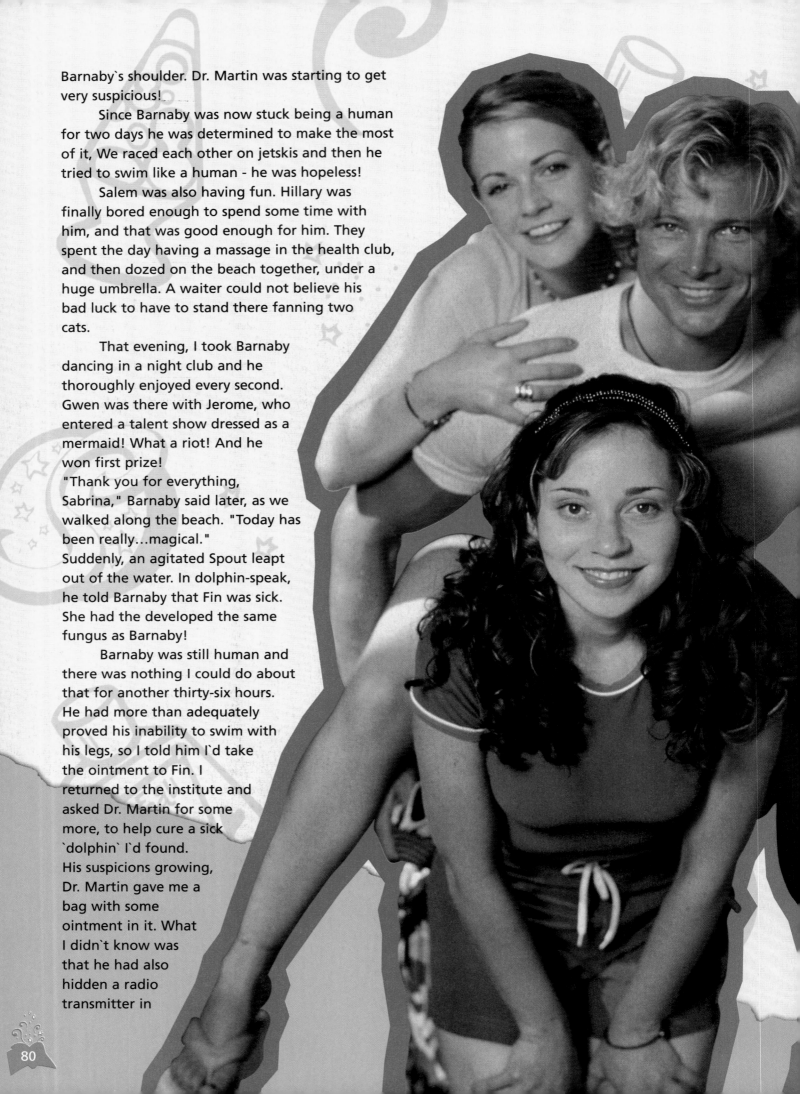

Barnaby`s shoulder. Dr. Martin was starting to get very suspicious!

Since Barnaby was now stuck being a human for two days he was determined to make the most of it, We raced each other on jetskis and then he tried to swim like a human - he was hopeless!

Salem was also having fun. Hillary was finally bored enough to spend some time with him, and that was good enough for him. They spent the day having a massage in the health club, and then dozed on the beach together, under a huge umbrella. A waiter could not believe his bad luck to have to stand there fanning two cats.

That evening, I took Barnaby dancing in a night club and he thoroughly enjoyed every second. Gwen was there with Jerome, who entered a talent show dressed as a mermaid! What a riot! And he won first prize!

"Thank you for everything, Sabrina," Barnaby said later, as we walked along the beach. "Today has been really…magical."

Suddenly, an agitated Spout leapt out of the water. In dolphin-speak, he told Barnaby that Fin was sick. She had the developed the same fungus as Barnaby!

Barnaby was still human and there was nothing I could do about that for another thirty-six hours. He had more than adequately proved his inability to swim with his legs, so I told him I`d take the ointment to Fin. I returned to the institute and asked Dr. Martin for some more, to help cure a sick `dolphin` I`d found. His suspicions growing, Dr. Martin gave me a bag with some ointment in it. What I didn`t know was that he had also hidden a radio transmitter in the bag so that he could track my every move!

I ran back down to the dock and took hold of Spout. I gotta tell you, dolphins are the only way to travel! He swam me far out to a beautiful lagoon, where I found a colony of mermaids and mermen. They all hid in the water when they saw me, terrified of humans, but finally I convinced Fin to make an appearance and let me put the medicine on her.

"Fine," she grumbled. "But if I somehow end up with legs, you`re in a lot of trouble."

However, she quickly began to trust me, and even invited me to have something to eat. She held up a live squid and bit off its head.

"They`re delicious," she said. I`ll take her word for that!

Unfortunately, the radio transmitter in my bag was sending back the location of the lagoon to Dr. Martin.

"No one goes there," said his assistant as they scoured maps of the Reef. "That lagoon is completely inaccessible to boats."

But if I could get there, Dr. Martin was determined that he would, too!

Early next morning, a love-stricken Salem took Hillary to the look out point on the other side of the island, to watch a spectacular sunrise.

"Oh, Salem," purred Hillary. "It`s glorious."

Salem had brought along a camera with him. He started clicking away, unaware of a ship not too far off the shore. As the sun rose, bathing the island in a warm red glow, Salem and Hillary came together and kissed!

In our bungalow, Gwen and I were getting dressed. Barnaby would be turning back into a merman later that day, and I wanted to be there to see him off.

Looking in the bag Dr. Martin had given me, I was horrified to discover the radio transmitter. I knew immediately what that meant. He had tracked my movements the day before.

"Then he knows where the colony is," groaned Gwen.

I went looking for Dr. Martin, but the institute was empty. Salem and Hillary were at the resort grounds on which the institute was located, looking over the pictures Salem had taken.

"I heard your doctor friend talk about storming some lagoon this morning," Hillary told me. "He was quite full of himself."

Horrified, I started for the dock, then noticed something in one of Salem's pictures. I grabbed the photo and ran to stop Dr. Martin. I got to him just as he was about to sail off in his boat.

"Please," I pleaded with him. "You don`t know what you`re doing."

"I know more about this reef than you could ever hope to know," snorted Dr. Martin. "If there`s something out there, I`m going to find it."

With that, he set sail - I had to stop him!

Barnaby and Gwen came running up. "What are you just standing here for?" cried Barnaby, in panic. "You have to do something."

Barnaby ran up to the look out point to keep watch on his home and Dr. Martin getting closer and closer to it. Gwen and I stood at the edge of the water trying to come up with a plan. I decided to use a weather spell, but Gwen was worried because they could be pretty dangerous.

I had no choice. I shouted out the spell, took a deep breath and blew. Immediately the wind picked up and ominous black clouds appeared. Thunder rumbled!

Out at sea, the wind howled ferociously. Rain lashed down. The waves grew higher.

"We can`t take this kind of weather," Dr. Martin's assistant shouted. "We have to turn around." The doctor was not pleased.

"See, nothing to it," I said to Gwen. "I don`t know what you were so worried…"

ZZZZAAP! A huge bolt of lightning hit the water near me. I was thrown back onto the beach, unconscious!

You knew this was serious because Salem left Hillary and joined Barnaby to rush to my side.

"Oh, please," pleaded Gwen, shaking her fist. "Just this once."

Gwen and I disappeared back to the bungalow.

"Oh, thank goodness," gasped Gwen, remembering what happened in Rome, and pretty much any time she tried to send someone somewhere. "We`re not in Greenland."

Barnaby and Salem jumped into Dr. Martin`s pick-up truck to follow us. Being a merman, Barnaby had never driven before, and Salem couldn't take the wheel for obvious reasons. As the truck lurched forward, Barnaby madly swung the steering wheel back and forth, the vehicle swerving across the road.

"Just my luck," groaned Salem. "I meet the woman of my dreams and I die in a fiery car wreck."

They sped towards the institute, and just as they arrived, Barnaby turned back into a merman, complete with giant fish`s tail!

Unable to see where he was going, Barnaby desperately spun the wheel and the truck screeched to a stop, almost knocking down the returning Dr. Martin.

Dr. Martin ran over and yanked open the driver`s side door. Barnaby flopped out onto the ground in front of him.

"Hey, doc," said Barnaby, flapping his tail. "Shoulder`s doing a lot better."

Salem rushed back to find me. I had recovered somewhat from my shock, although my magic would be out of whack for a few hours. Gwen and I had gone down to the dock to see what had happened. Salem told us that Dr. Martin had captured Barnaby and had him locked up in the resort`s swimming pool.

Before I could react, Fin appeared. I had to tell her the whole, unfortunate, terrible story.

"Barnaby was a fool to have trusted you," she said. "Let`s hope I can save the rest of us." She flipped over in the water and swam away. Things were definitely not going according to plan!

The manager of the resort, alerted to Dr. Martin`s find, had already contacted all the news organisations. Helicopters were flying over the resort, trying to get photographs of Dr. Martin`s mysterious discovery. Reporters crowded the lobby, interviewing Dr. Martin as I burst through.

"Who`s the poacher now, Dr. Martin?" I hissed, before angrily storming off.

Seeing Gwen with Jerome, I suddenly had an idea.

"What are you shiela`s lookin` at me so funny for?" asked Jerome, as Gwen grinned, realising what I had in mind. We each grabbed an arm and pulled him along.

A guard had been put on the swimming pool to stop anyone from seeing Barnaby. While Salem distracted him, Gwen and I sneaked past and pulled Barnaby onto a room service cart.

In his place, we left a bemused and confused Jerome decked out in his prize-winning mermaid costume.

Not wanting to exploit Barnaby (just study him like some science experiment….harumph!), Dr. Martin refused to let anyone visit the swimming pool. The hotel manager insisted though, wanting the publicity for himself. But thanks to our quick thinking, when the reporters arrived, all they found was Jerome, strumming a ukulele.

"Is this your idea of a joke?" exploded the manager towards Dr. Martin.

"Sabrina," growled the doctor, figuring out my plan. "Wait here. We`ll be right back."

And, he headed for the dock!

Pushing the service cart down a steep hill, Barnaby holding on for dear life, I spotted Dr. Martin and his boat crew chasing towards us!
I gave the cart one final push and it hurtled towards the end. It smacked into a post, catapulting Barnaby through the air. He made a perfect dive into the water! SPLASH!

Unfortunately, Dr. Martin had already set sail in his boat. He began throwing nets into the water…and soon had poor Barnaby recaptured!

At just the right moment Spout appeared. I dove into the water and took hold of the dolphin. I told Gwen to meet me over at the doctor's boat.

Thinking she was on a roll with her magic after the last time, Gwen clenched her fist. She disappeared…and missed the deck of the boat by a couple of metres.

"Oh, frizzle," she groaned, plummeting into the water with a SPLASH!

I arrived to find Fin trying to rescue her brother from the net. Asking Spout to go and find something for me, deep down in the reef, I beckoned to a soaking wet Gwen to follow me onto the boat.

Climbing aboard without anyone seeing us, we unhooked part of the net trapping Barnaby. He was free!

"Game`s over, Sabrina," said Dr. Martin, spotting us. "You`re very clever, but no one makes a fool of me on my reef."

He helped his crew pull in the net, lifting it clear of the water, believing they still had Barnaby captured. But it was Fin!

"Sabrina?" sobbed Fin, looking up at me. "What`s happening?! Why are you doing this?"

Without my magic, I had no chance of saving the mer-people. I didn`t know what else to do!

And then the cavalry arrived, in the form of Spout! He had found what I had asked. He flicked it into the air for me to catch. It was the blue spot butterfly fish.

"Incredible," gasped Dr. Martin when he saw it. But he was still adamant about capturing the mer-people.

I demanded to know what he was trying to protect. His ego? His reputation?

Grabbing a knife from the sheath on Dr. Martin`s belt, I started cutting through the rope holding the net.

Dr. Martin forcibly grabbed hold of my wrist. "Drop the knife," he snarled. "I`m not going to let you destroy the greatest discovery of the century."

"And I`m not going to let you destroy their lives," I snapped. "This reef doesn`t belong to you. It belongs to them. By the way, how does it feel to be on the other side?"

My words struck home. Dr. Martin realised he was no better than the poachers he had stopped a few days earlier.

"Not good," he said, releasing me. I cut the final strand, and Fin dropped back into the water. She and Barnaby swam away.

I told Dr. Martin that I knew he would never let anyone hurt a living creature on the reef. He`d dedicated his whole life to the ocean.

"And what do I have to show for it?" he asked.

I looked out across the magnificent Great Barrier Reef.

"Everything," I said.

"Everything," agreed Dr. Martin. "Can`t really ask for much more than that now, can I?"

Thanks to the discovery of the blue spot butterfly fish, Dr. Martin was able by law to cordon off the entire eastern half of the island, and reclassify it as a preservation zone. Entry into the area would be completely forbidden, except for scientific research. The mer-people would be safe again. We had won! Woo hoo!

But it was Boo Hoo for Salem. He'd lost his chance for true love when Hillary changed back from a cat into a woman. She had taken the trip to celebrate the end of her sentence as a cat. Unfortunately, Salem had another 87 years to go until he returned to human form – and that was with good behaviour!

"Salem, this is good-bye," she told him. "I`m really more of a dog person."

Poor Salem was heartbroken. He actually began to whimper!

However, the mysterious `Mr. Saberhagen` was praised for his dedicated efforts to help

protect the reef. Remember that picture I had grabbed from him before? In the background of the shot, Salem had managed to capture the ship that had been contaminating the waters. "Mr. Saberhagen" had turned the pictures over to the authorities and arrests had been made!

Listening to all this at a press conference, Salem sat on the lap of a very attractive woman.

"Oh, you are just the cutest little thing," she said, stroking him. Salem purred loudly, Hillary already forgotten. True love, eh?

When everything had quieted down, Gwen and I returned to Barnaby and Fin's cove. What better way to end a spectacular vacation, and what better tour guides to the magnificent Great Barrier Reef?

Find That

Have fun being a mermaid in this exciting game for two or more players. You will need a dice and counters. See who will be first to swim through the Great Barrier Reef and find the hidden treasure!

2

Caught in a fisherman's net. Miss a turn.

5

Dolphin shows you short cut. Move on 5 squares.

7

1

4

8

Seaquake scares you back 4 places.

10

11

12

Water turns freezing cold. Hurry on 2 squares.

17

14

15

Fight an octopus. Miss 2 turns.

Treasure!

29

Find sunken pirates ship. Hurry on 2 places.

28

Shark attack! Go back 3 places.

31

26

32

25

Discover underwater city. Move on 3 places.

Divers try to catch you. Go back 4 places.

24

22

34

18

Foot trapped in coral. Miss a turn.

19

21

36

Lose your way. Go back 3 squares.

Dolphin Paperweight

Sabrina and I had a great time in Australia - the Great barrier Reef is awesome! And Spout was so cute! Wanna make a dolphin paperweight? (They make great presents for family and friends!) Then follow the instructions below!

You will need

230g of non-bake modelling clay (you can buy this in any craft shop).

Sheet of thick card and tracing paper.

Flat-ended knife and round-ended scissors.

Damp sponge.

Tin of varnish.

Poster paint (grey or light blue)

Thin paintbrush.

Stick of PVA glue.

Small sequin button and silver glitter.

Copy this dolphin stencil onto tracing paper, and transfer onto the card. Cut out the dolphin shape (or ask a grown-up to help). Roll the clay into a ball to soften up.

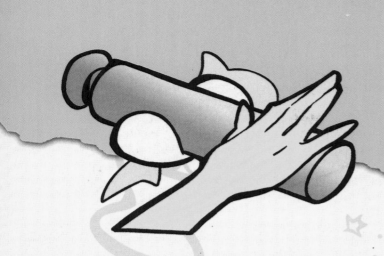

Place the clay-ball onto your stencil. Use a rolling pin to roll out the clay until it is approximately 2.5cm thick. (The rolling pin will help keep the stencil in place.)

Carefully cut around the stencil with a flat-ended knife. Use a damp sponge to smooth the surface and edges of your clay dolphin-shape.

Make fine lines with the knife on the clay model for the dolphin's mouth, neck, fin and tail. Leave to dry and harden overnight.

Paint your dolphin-shape with poster paints, leave to dry and then varnish. (For a glittery effect, you could sprinkle silver glitter onto the shape.) Once the varnish has dried, use PVA glue and a small sequin button for the dolphin's eye.

And now you have your own cool dolphin paperweight!

It's A Mad, Mad, Mad, Mad Season

**Original story written
by Holly Hester**

Dashiell`s the name, and charmin` ladies is my game! Well, one lady in particular. Sabrina Spellman.
And since I`m a young guy from the Other Realm, I had a pretty good chance of putting her under my spell of luuurrrvvve!

There was just one problem. Harvey Kinkle. A mortal Sabrina still had some major feelings for. Now, Sabrina and Harvey weren`t going steady when I met her, so she was happy to go out with me a few times. We really had fun and I thought we could get serious. It was time for her to choose her one true love.

Harvey didn`t know I was a warlock, but he did recognise competition when he saw it.

After one of *their* dates, he cuddled, gave her one of his love-sick looks, and told her what a great time he had had with her.

"Harvey," scolded Sabrina. "You`re doing it again."

"Sorry," he said. "I`m just wondering if you've made any decisions about the me-or-Dashiell-my-short-life-will-come-to-an-abrupt-end-if-you-don`t-pick-me-situation?"

That`s when I appeared on the living room couch, as if by magic, and presented Sabrina with a beautiful bouquet of flowers.

"So who`s it going to be?" I asked a flustered Sabrina. "Me or, er..." I turned to Harvey. "I`m sorry, I forgot your name." And you thought you girls were catty!

Before Sabrina could answer, Harvey

and I (so Sabrina told me later) were frozen by her Aunt Zelda and Aunt Hilda who arrived and very excitedly handed Sabrina an envelope.

"Sabrina Spellman," she read. "Please join us for a ceremony tomorrow honouring you for receiving your Witches` Licence!"

The three of them jumped around, screaming like little girls. The day Sabrina had waited for all this time had finally arrived. She was going to become a fully-licenced witch!

Sabrina, knew enough about the Other Realm to know everthing came with a catch.

"No catch," explained Aunt Hilda. "And once you get your Witches` Licence a world of power and knowledge will automatically be within you."

Great, thought Sabrina. Then she`d be able to choose between me and Harvey!

Life got even better for Sabrina at Westbridge High the following day. The school had ranked number one in the country on school board exams, so the Principal had decided to hold a dance for all the students that coming Friday evening. And since Sabrina had done particularly well, she would get to choose the theme of the dance. The only stipulation being it had to be based on a favourite movie.

Of course, both Harvey and I asked her to be our date, but she couldn`t make up her mind. "You`ll have to wait until tomorrow," she explained, hoping that getting her Witches' Licence would help her decide. "I`ll know so much more about everything tomorrow."

Mr Kraft, the school`s Vice Principal, phoned Sabrina`s aunts later that evening to ask if they would chaperone the dance. Aunt Hilda couldn't stand him. but she knew Mr. Kraft had a crush on her, and she dreaded he would ask her to the dance. Aunt Zelda solved the problem by offering to beat him to the punch by asking him to go with her. Turns out she found the weasly Vice Principal attractive. Go figure.

At school the next day, Sabrina told Mr Kraft that she was thinking maybe `Saturday night Fever` or `Grease` as the movie theme for the dance. Mr Kraft had never heard of either of them! He was thinking more of *his* favourite film, `Billy Jack`, a flick no one else had ever heard of.

Having overheard the

conversation, I tried to make points. When Sabrina opened her locker door, she found a miniature me dressed a la John Travolta dancing to loud disco music. And I`ve got all the moves!

That evening, Sabrina looked beautiful in the dress she chose to attend the ceremony for her Witches` Licence. Exiting the linen closet in the Other Realm, she was disappointed to find that instead of an elegant ball, she was stuck in line at the Witches' Licence Bureau your typical, drab government office.

"Hi, there must be some mistake," she told the dour clerk behind the counter. "I was supposed to be sent to a party for my Witches` Licence. My name is Sabrina Spellman."

The clerk checked her computer. "Nope. You`re in the right place."

"But it can`t be!" groaned Sabrina, her heart sinking. "It`s supposed to be this huge celebration."

Remember our girl thought there would be a catch? Well, here it was. It turned out that before she could get her licence, she had one final test. Luckily, it was an easy one. Sabrina gave the correct answer, and bam! her license was rubber stamped by the clerk. The government office suddenly transformed into a plush ballroom, filled with elegantly-dressed party-goers!

"Now this is more like it!" cheered Sabrina.

Aunt Zelda and Aunt Hilda arrived to share the moment with her. And the clerk - who`s name was Doris turned out to be one of Sabrina`s many cousins.

When Doris took Sabrina's picture for her licence, our teenage witch wasn't at all happy with the results. Sabrina tried to get a re-take, but all she got was the gooey end of Doris' quick temper. Seems when Doris got angry, she shot goo out of her fingertips! And let me tell you, there is no such thing as good goo.

Moving on - who has a good picture on their licence after all - Sabrina was just happy to finally get her licence after having the prospect dangled in front of her for a year. And, now literally dangling in front of her at her party. But when she tried to grab it, she got a painful electric shock!

Catch Number Two: "Before a witch can use their licence, they have to discover their family secret," explained Aunt Zelda.

It seems that this secret would break the spell on the licence and then Sabrina would be free to use it. Periodically, family members would visit her to serve as her guide. Doris would be the first to visit.

Sabrina couldn't believe it! No "world of power and knowledge" automatically within her. That meant she would have to decide between Harvey and me on her own. Like a normal teenager!

"Well, this just…stinks!" groaned Sabrina.

Harvey and I made things even harder for her. Both tired of waiting, we told her at school that if she didn't decide by the following day, she wouldn't get either of us.

"And not just for the dance," said Harvey forcefully. "Forever."

Hey, guys don't like to be kept waiting, all right?!

On top of everything else, Mr Kraft was still waiting for her choice for the dance theme. He'd dispatched Sabrina's best friend, Val, to get an answer. But, Sabrina had too much on her mind to worry about that too.

"Just make it 'Grease'," she said. And, that was that.

Back home, Salem was sending a rude e-mail to an Albanian potato farmer named Yuri who had beaten him at Internet chess.

And Hilda was sulking because even though she didn't like Mr. Kraft, she liked that he liked her. It was good for her self-esteem. But, now that he knew Zelda liked him, would he stop liking her? Could she cope? There's never a dull day in that house!

Panicked over who should be her date for the dance, Sabrina turned for help to Salem, who suggested she try a spell from the magic book.

Flipping through the `love` section, she found a spell that would give her a physical manifestation of her feelings. "It says here that if I use this spell correctly," she read out to Salem, "my heart will be revealed to me. Sounds gory." But Salem told her it would just show her heart's true desire. So, hand over heart, she began to sing out the spell…

ask yourself, are you feeling lucky?"

"I`ve always been lucky," I sneered back.

We circled each other, ready for a bloody shoot-out.

Just then, Mr Kraft appeared, and a panicking Sabrina pushed him down a side corridor so he didn`t see the gunfight. He started to complain about her film choice for the dance, when they both heard galloping horses hooves echoing down the hallways.

"Funny," said Mr Kraft, rather confused. "I don`t remember this school having a blacksmith."

When Sabrina looked again, we had both gone. She rushed through the school, eventually finding us in the cafeteria. Now we were both dressed in fencing suits and masks. The fencing swords we were holding clashed together as we fought to the death!

Sabrina tried to diffuse the confusion by laughing it off, "Those 'drama students' sure need a lot of attention," she said somewhat unconvincingly.

Sabrina chased after us, but we were nowhere to be seen.

Mr Kraft tried to catch up with her, only to be waylaid by Aunt Hilda, who was acting extremely out of character. She said she wanted to discuss going to the dance on Friday. Mr Kraft explained that Aunt Zelda had already asked him.

"She did?" pouted Aunt Hilda, pretending not to know. "Well, fiddlesticks on her. How dare she take my man away from me!"

Mr Kraft was genuinely shocked. He didn`t

The next day at school, Sabrina heard the sound of jingling spurs. Not a sound you usually hear in a high school hallway. She turned to see Harvey and I at each opposite end of the corridor, wearing cowboy outfits and Stetsons. We both wore gun belts, our hands twitching beside the handles of our six-guns. This was gonna be the final showdown!

"Oh, no!" groaned Sabrina. "This must be the spell. They`re going to fight over my heart. Being a witch would be a lot easier without all this magic."

"So, Dashiell," sneered Harvey. "You gotta

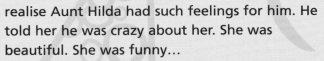

realise Aunt Hilda had such feelings for him. He told her he was crazy about her. She was beautiful. She was funny…

"Thanks," said Aunt Hilda, returning to normal. "That's all I wanted to know." She'd had her fix of self-esteem, and she was good to go. Heading out she saw me and Harvey, now dressed as Ninjas, battling in the corridor, performing kung-fu kicks, and somehow speaking Japanese. Badly, I might add. Hilda pointed Sabrina in our direction.

She pleaded with us to stop, but it was no use. The spell was in full-force. Sabrina was about as stressed as I'd ever seen her, and things didn't get any better when Cousin Doris appeared to talk about the Spellman family secret.

"Doris," groaned Sabrina. "There are two ninjas fighting to the death for my love in the middle of my high school! Now is not a good time."

Oooh, boy! That made Doris angry. Very, very angry! Gooey finger angry. She released a huge glop of the sticky green stuff from her fingertips right in our direction!

"Harvey!" cried Sabrina, pushing him out of the way of Doris's attack. He crashed to the ground, knocked unconscious. I, meanwhile, was splattered in goo! Thank you very much.

"Well," said Doris, calming down. "It looks like you're busy. I'll come back later." And with that, she vanished.

"Dashiell, I'm sorry," apologised Sabrina, rushing over to me. "I guess I couldn't get to you in time."

But I knew better. "My big brother warned me about this spell," I said, sadly. "You jumped in front of Harvey because he's the one your heart chose."

"Wow," said Sabrina. "So the spell really did work. I'm sorry."

So was I, but what could I do? Her heart had

spoken. I told Sabrina that I`d still like us to be friends and she was cool with that. I left to soothe my wounded ego and de-goo the rest of me. I believe it was then that Sabrina asked a rather confused Harvey to take her to the dance!

When Friday came, Aunt Hilda was at home with Salem, unable to face going to the dance without a date. The doorbell rang, and outside was a rather angry, rather large man in a sheepskin coat, fur hat and Cossack boots.

"I am Yuri," he growled. "I come to kill Salem." It was the Albanian potato farmer to whom Salem had been sending rude e-mails! "Salem has insulted my mother for last time. I will wear his entrails as hat."

Aunt Hilda saved Salem's fur and her pride by taking Yuri to the school dance.

"I didn`t do it for you," she told Salem after she had pushed Yuri back outside and Salem had thanked her. "I need a date, and underneath all those pelts it looks like he`s got a pretty good body."

Inside the high school gym, the `Grease` theme dance was in full swing, rock `n` roll music blaring out. Sabrina and Harvey were Westbridge's very own, very perfect Sandy and Danny.

"Will you go steady with me again?" Harvey asked Sabrina, as they danced to a romantic song.

"Really?" smiled Sabrina happily. "I`d love to."

What can I say? Those two really were made for each other!

Dressing-Up Sabrina!

Hi, everyone! Aunt Zelda and Aunt Hilda here. Can you help us design two dresses for Sabrina? One is for the ball she`s attending after receiving her Witches` Licence, and the other is for her Fifties` high school dance!

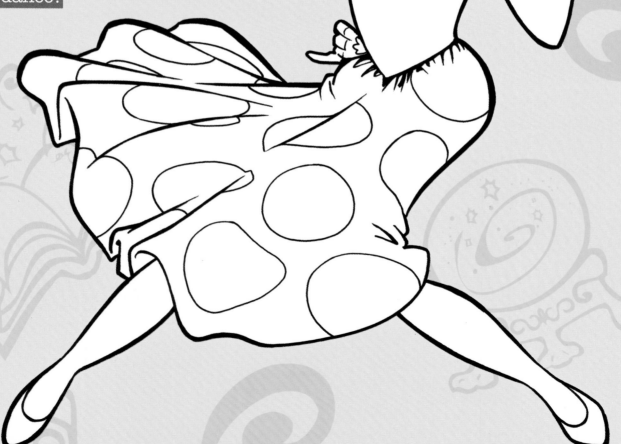

You can colour in the dresses with coloured pencils or crayons, and decorate them with sticky shapes or glitter sticks. (Just remember not to shut the annual until the glue has dried!) Once you`ve finished the dresses, we`re sure Sabrina will think they`re both `magic`!

Original story written by Betsy Borns

Prelude To A Kiss

Salem here, fur-fans, with a final tale about the world`s goofiest teenage witch.
Everything changes when you turn eighteen. And it sure did for Sabrina!

She finally had her Witch's Licence - she was now a fully-fledged witch! The Witches' Council, in its infinite wisdom (NOT!), decided that she should mentor Dreama, another teenage witch, who had yet to get her licence.

Dreama had been neglecting her magic, and her parents moved her to Westbridge from the Other Realm so that Sabrina could help her.

Sabrina also had an after-school job at a coffee house. The place was managed by a guy named Josh, and Sabrina had a major crush on him. Although, we probably shouldn't tell Harvey that!

I was busy practising the martial arts programme of Tae-Bo - instead of conquering the world, I had decided I was just gonna kick butt! - and Aunt Hilda and Aunt Zelda were busy cleaning the house, for the first time in about 150 years, when Sabrina and Dreama, came home one afternoon.

"Aunt Hilda. Aunt Zelda," said Sabrina anxiously. "Take a look at this." She nodded to Dreama. "Go ahead, Turn the bowl into an apple."

Dreama tugged at her ear (hey, not all witches point, y`know!), concentrating on a fruit bowl on the sideboard. It shrank in size, turning into a rosy red apple. Perfect!

The trouble was, the spell only lasted a few seconds before returning back into a bowl again.

"This keeps happening," Sabrina explained. "I think it`s because she`s nervous. Remember when I used to get nervous and all I could zap in were pineapples?"

"But never the ham," I sighed.

But, I digress. Sabrina and Harvey`s relationship was going through a `bad spell` (sorry, couldn`t resist!)...they seemed to be drifting further and further apart. Harvey expected Sabrina to attend every football game, even though in all his years at Westbridge High and being on the team, he had never actually played in a game.
And since his best bud, Brad, moved back, Sabrina hardly ever saw him *unless* he was on the bench at a game. They were growing apart. Which is better than growing a tail, trust me.

"We don`t have to be together on every date," she sighed after one of Harvey's games. He'd agreed to have coffee with her, but she knew he really wanted to go play football with his friends. Being the good girlfriend that she was, Sabrina told him to do what he wanted.

"Man, we have a great relationship," said Harvey, oblivious to Sabrina's disappointment.

The next day, Sabrina was back at the coffee house, but as a worker, not a customer. She was cleaning tables with Josh, when he told her he had a big exam coming up. Sabrina fibbed, and told him she knew all about the subject - `Oliver Twist` and one ping and one spell later, she did. Well, one ping, one pineapple and one spell later. I think Josh made her a little nervous. Or, maybe that should be liking Josh made her a little nervous. In any case, Sabrina spent the rest of the evening quizzing Josh for his test, and enjoying every minute of their time together. The little Dickens!

While Sabrina was flirting with Josh (you didn't hear that from mee...oww), Aunt Zelda and Aunt Hilda had had it with the housework. They sent a request to the Other Realm for a house-keeper. What they got were the three pirates thay'd accidentally locked in the attic (and only discovered decades later). The pirates charged out of the linen closet with a hearty "Arrgghh" and a hefty feather duster.

"I want a word with that agency," exclaimed Aunt Zelda.

After school the next day, Sabrina asked Harvey if they were going to do their usual aimless Thursday ritual of wandering around the shopping mall. But Harvey had other plans.

Some of the guys were going to kidnap Eastbridge`s football mascot before the next big match and they needed him to come along.

"Why?" asked Sabrina, noticeably annoyed. "How many people does it take to steal a turtle?"

Dreama walked over to Sabrina as Harvey stormed off. "Are you okay?" she asked.

"Totally!" Sabrina snapped. "That`s the kind of relationship Harvey and I have. He does what he wants to do, and I do what I want to do and we`re both so mature we don`t even care that we`re not seeing each other."

Returning home after a day working in their new clock store (don't ask!), Aunt Zelda and Aunt Hilda were really worried about what they might find.

"I hope the pirates are having a good day," said Aunt Zelda.

"Or at least a bloodless one," agreed Aunt Hilda.

They were delighted to find that the pirates had been working hard. The house definitely looked a lot better.

"Nice job, boys," said Aunt Zelda, pleased with what she saw.

While Harvey was off turtle stealing, Sabrina went to work at the coffee house. Josh said he was really grateful for her help with "Oliver Twist" - he'd ace his exams. He then asked Sabrina for help on another book. Josh said he could schedule the study session for Friday night, if she could.

Without thinking, Sabrina agreed. It had felt so good to be appreciated for a change. But Dreama reminded her that she had promised to watch Harvey's football game Friday night.

"I forgot," Sabrina groaned. "Oh, Harvey won`t mind. He never even notices me there. He won`t care if I skip it just once."

Then Harvey came in. He gave Sabrina a present...a `Beat Eastbridge` t-shirt. He said it was going to be the best game ever.

Then Aunt Hilda opened a closet...and out fell the mailman, the newspaper boy, an Avon lady and a flower delivery man!

"Who are these people?" gasped Aunt Zelda.

"Scurvy knaves what come to pillage," growled the pirate called Blackbeard.

"Anyone who rang the doorbell," explained his mate Nemo.

"Okay, maybe this game does mean a little something to Harvey," sighed Sabrina. "I`ll just talk to Josh."

Before she had the chance, Josh thanked her again and told her that the next test counted for half his grade.

Sabrina was, as usual, in the middle of a mess of her own making.

Sabrina came home, desperate for help with her Harvey/Josh problem. Being a Tae Bo master, I listened calmly to her dilemma, then nodded sagely. "And in this scenario, who do you need to kick-box?" I asked.

But, the girl just can't hold a train of thought. Not a natural for the Eastern arts like yours truly; one minute she's whining about her boy troubles and the next she asks, "Do I smell fudge?"

Fudge? I ask you what does, fudge...wait, I smelled it too. How did I miss that? The pirates had been in the kitchen, making fudge. Sabrina stuffed her face (none for me, thanks, I'm in training - and nobody offered!), and they discussed her choices. Josh would be inconvenienced but Harvey would be hurt. So Sabrina decided that when she got to work that night, she would tell Josh that she couldn't help him study.

But, before Sabrina could give Josh the bad news, he spoke first. He explained that he was on a scholarship and if he didn't keep his grades up, it'd be gone. So was Sabrina sure she didn't mind helping him?

"Please," said Sabrina with as much sincerity as she could muster. "Like I've got somewhere else to be?"

And the good news just kept comin'. Harvey ran into the coffee house excitedly! So many of his teammates were sick, there was a real possibility that he might get to play.
"How lucky is that?" beamed Harvey. "I might actually get into the game before I graduate! And my best girl will get to see it."

"Yeah, how lucky is that?" Sabrina said with a little less sincerity this time.

Never one to give up in the face of adversity, Sabrina came up with a plan. Dreama would go to Harvey's game, and if he played, she could witch-page Sabrina who would zap back from studying with Josh. I should mention that Dreama has no idea how the game of football is played. But, this didn't stop our Sabrina.

She handed Dreama a witch-pager, and warned her not to use it frivolously because it was on vibrate and Sabrina was very ticklish.

So Dreama went to the game, and Sabrina went to the coffee house to study with Josh.

Aunt Zelda and Aunt Hilda were at home enjoying a special dinner the pirates had prepared as a way of saying thanks for hiring them. The dishes were very "pirate-y" except for the crème brulée dessert...that the pirates had plundered form our neighbour! Well, you can't really refine a pirate overnight, I guess.

Dreama was watching the football game when she saw Harvey stand up from the bench. Thinking he was playing she held up the witch-pager and tugged on her ear. In the coffee house, her own witch-pager vibrating in her trouser pocket, Sabrina suddenly burst out laughing. This perplexed Josh`s friends, who had stopped by to share some Chinese food.

But, Sabrina couldn't worry about that now. She rushed out back and pointed at herself. Next moment, she was standing beside Dreama, only to be told Harvey had stood up just to get some water. So back she went to the coffee house.

Again and again, Harvey made a movement which Dreama took to mean he was playing in the game, and Sabrina zapped back and forth so many times it was starting to look suspicius. When she tried to point up something that would

justify her many trips to the bathroom (well, she couldn't disappear right in front of everybody), all she got were pineapples. Yup, Josh was definitely making her nervous - or maybe it was deceiving Harvey. Whatever it was, she never came up with a good excuse for those pineapples. And may I say, still no ham to go with them. Some things never change.

Josh`s friends gave Josh a quizzical look after Sabrina had disappeared for the third time.

"I like her," said Josh, defensively. Give the guy some credit for knowing a good thing when he sees it!

Eventually, Sabrina got so frustrated, she told Dreama she was turning off the witch-pager. There were only two minutes left in the game, and she was sure Harvey wouldn`t be playing.

But moments after she had disappeared back to the coffee shop, one of the Westbridge High players got injured, and Harvey was in. For the first time ever!

"Yey!" cheered Dreama, but then realised she couldn`t call Sabrina back. "Booo!" she groaned.

And it got worse. Not only did Harvey play, he scored a touchdown, turning the game from a humiliating loss for his team into a...well, less humiliating loss!

Receiving slaps and cheers from his teammates, Harvey shrugged them aside as he headed for the bleachers to celebrate with Sabrina.

"Please let this work," prayed Dreama, tugging on her ear before transforming into a Sabrina lookalike. A smiling Harvey climbed over the barrier, heading for `Sabrina`, when one of

his teammates called up to him.

Looking back down to the field, he failed to see Dreama`s magic come unstuck again as she changed back to her normal self!

"Where did Sabrina go?" Harvey asked Dreama, reaching her.

"She had to go home," said Dreama, thinking quickly. "She was...sick!"

Harvey hurried off to get changed, so that he could visit his `sick` girlfriend and make sure she was okay!

Meantime, Aunt Hilda and Aunt Zelda had decided to give the pirates some good news. They were going to hire them permanently! It came as a bit of a shock to find that the pirates didn`t want the job!

"With all of our skills." announced Hook. "We need to work for people who have taste and breeding."

"Someone classy." added Nemo. Can you belive these guys? The drama inside couldn't match the drama outside the house tonight, though. Josh had walked Sabrina. He thanked her for her help, and leaned forward to kiss her on the cheek. Then their lips met! Sabrina closed her eyes, savouring the moment.

"You don`t look sick to me," said a dejected Harvey, appearing beside them .

"Harvey, wait!" cried Sabrina, as Harvey stormed off.

Oops! But as you know, after many ups and downs, Sabrina and Harvey did patch things up and got back together. After all, they were soul mates!

Having A

Salem and I love having competitions to see who can tell the best jokes. Who`s jokes do you think are the funniest?

What do you get when you cross a werewolf with a vampire?

A fur coat that fangs around your neck!

How do ghosts fly on holiday?

By Scareplane!

How do scary witches keep their hair out of place?

With scare spray!

What do you get when you cross a vampire with a snowman?

Frostbite!

Laugh!

What does the daddy ghost say to his family when driving?

Fasten your sheet belts!

What do you call two witches who share a room?

Broom-mates!

Why do mummies have trouble keeping friends?

They`re too wrapped up in themselves!

What`s a zombie`s favourite street?

A dead-end street!

109